ARTISITIC
ENDEAVORS

Table of Contents

CHOICES 1
EXPERIMENTATION 11
A TRIP IN THE PRESENT 27
BACK TO THE GALLERY 39
IN THE PAST 48
IN THE PRESENT 55
FRESCO 61
MONET 70
PAST TO THE PRESENT 76
FUTURE TO THE PAST 84
DUPLICITY 93
TREACHERY 102
EXEGESIS 112
RETRIBUTION 121
TWO TO ONE 129
RESCUE ATTEMPT 137
PLANS AND PROMISES 144
RESOLUTION 152
PROSPECTS.. 159
FINALE' 166

Dedicated to Tyler and Kaylee,
My reason to keep going through good times and bad.

CHOICES

Martin poised the hammer and chisel over the nose of a bust of Cassius. He just had a minor adjustment to make, then the bust would be finished. The chime of the doorbell startled him as the hammer came down with a heavy thwack. The nose dropped onto the floor. "Damn and blast it!" he kicked at the marble nose sending it rebounding off the wall. Angerly looking at the bust he had been carving. He raised the hammer. Holding the chisel against the defaced bust he smote the marble blow after blow. In a frenzy of frustration, he sent chips and chunks flying around the studio. Standing in the doorway Arthur dodged as a chunk whizzed past his ear.

Martin rounded on the intruder who had unintentionally caused the demolition of his latest piece. "What the hell do you want!" Arthur swallowed hard as he walked cautiously in. "Sorry for disturbing you Martin but we need to talk about that last set of sculptures you sent over." Martin grudgingly offered him a seat. Leaning back against the table he waited.

Arthur sat forward and tried to make his words persuasive, "Martin, these sculptures you're turning out are worthy of a place in a museum, but classical sculptures just don't sell well right now. I've told you before and I tell you again. You've got to go back to more innovative work. Those sell well enough to bring us both high profit. You've barely cleared the housekeeping with the ones you sent recently." Arthur shrugged and waited for an explosion from Martin.

Instead of the explosion, Martin sank onto a stool. "No, I guess you're right." He looked around sadly, "tell you what, I've got an idea for new piece, why don't I give you a call when it's ready and we can try this again." He rose and shook Arthurs hand. "I appreciate your trying to push my stuff. I've created plenty of pieces, but as you say, a lot haven't sold enough to do more than just get by. There's something missing in them, and I don't know what it is." He joined Arthur by his recent creations and seeing the disappointment writ plain upon his face swept those closest to the floor.

Arthur patted Martin on the shoulder, "Pal, we've known each other for a long time. In all that time all you have ever wanted to do was to create. When you do those combinations of sculpture and electronics it works, and you make bank. When you go back to these classical ones, not so close. But you're an artist to your marrow and I'll always be here to support you."

He stood up and put his jacket on. "One thing though, you might want to take a few anger management sessions with somebody." He zipped up his jacket, took a last swig of whiskey and drove over to the gallery to set up for its next exhibits.

Leaving the scattered marble to fend for itself Martin brushed off the worktable and brought out paper and pencil. The first sketch was of a similar bust to the one he had just destroyed. He stopped mid sketch; this wasn't what Arthur wanted. He had to get more creative if he wanted to eat.

The door burst open sending the bell clanging wildly. Leaping over the threshold Arthur went straight to one of the pieces by the wall. Reaching out he grabbed hold of a three-foot-high pedestal. It was capped with an oval plate with a large thin glass bottle resting on its side held in a sculpted wave. The thin glass was colored in various swirling shades of blue grey. Its delicacy was intriguing, he brought it to the light to examine it better. "Martin, I saw this one out of the corner of my eye, it didn't register though until a few seconds ago."

He joined his friend at the window as Arthur turned the piece around watching as the light changed the greys or blues intensity. "The play of light emphasizes some of the shades giving the piece a depth I hadn't noticed initially. It has a unique quality I think will sell well, why didn't you show me this one earlier?"

Martin relaxed, "It's an interesting piece all right. I was wondering what you'd think of it." He went to the desk and poured them both another stiff Martel Five Star that he kept for special occasions.

Arthur sipped the brandy appreciatively. "Martin, this is the one I'll give you space for!" He turned it slowly, "It has a subtlety, a finesse that is unique from your other classical works. I don't know how you achieved the swirling variations of blues and greys, but they are beautiful. It's a symphony in duality." He went on waxing enthusiastically on the piece, so much so that Martin suddenly burst out laughing. Arthur's brows shot up at his friends' merriment. "What's the joke?"

Martin slipped on some white cotton gloves and removed the bottle from the pedestal. The bottom had been cradled in a wave sculpted from foamed glass that had partially covered it. It was made to look as if the bottle had washed in from the sea. Bringing the underside into the light he pointed out an inscription. G.E. 8000-watt Acorn Lightbulb Serial Number 1137945x2.

Arthur was aghast, "It's a damned lightbulb for Christ sakes." He held the bulb and reexamined the markings. He laughed heartily. "You got me, I'm glad you stopped me in time from making a fool of myself. I would have gone on and on about it and then when someone bought it, we'd have been sued and my reputation as an expert shattered." He carefully replaced the bulb on its pedestal and carried it back to its place by the shelf." Still, it's almost a shame I can't put it on display. It is an attractive piece."

Passing a calendar hung on the shelf the date seeped imperceptibly into his brain. When sudden realization of the date came to the fore, he almost dropped the sculpture. He swung round on Martin. "I'm going to open space for this after all. I'm going all out too. This will be proclaimed as one of your greatest works to date. Rig up a light for it for the gallery and we'll stick it on display tomorrow with a starting bid on the ticket of five hundred. No, a thousand" Martin looked at his friend as if he had taken his last marble and thrown it contemptuously out the door and across the street.

"Arthur, I think you had to much Martel or else you are trying to get yourself and me thrown in jail for fraud." Arthur was now laughing so hard he staggered over to the chair and continued until he had gotten it out of his system. Leaning back weakly he pointed to the calendar. Once Martin saw that April Fool's Day was a week away, he joined in the laughter. Suddenly he sobered up. "Yeah, but what if someone wants to buy it?"

Arthur considered this and his grin broadened. "If someone wants it, we sell it. However, we'll explain this was an April Fool's joke and show them the bottom. If they still want it, well by explaining about it were off the hook and you take the money, minus the galleries commission of course." He watched as Martin nervously wiped his hands on a drop cloth. "Martin, you're thinking too much about the fact it's a bulb. Remember Duchamp entered a urinal into an art show once just by putting a number on it and calling it a fountain?"

Arthur took plenty of pictures and went back to the gallery with the role of film and his notes. Martin placed the pedestal near the table and began creating a lighting source. When completed it would represent the sun beating down on the beach the bottle was cast up on. He tried bulb after bulb until he found one bright enough to show the shading off but not so bright as to lose everything in the glare. A new thought struck him. He cut the light cord and stuck in a dimmer switch. This way it became changeable emphasizing whatever the viewer wanted.

He brought out some foam wrap and covered everything reenforcing things with cardboard. Tape held it together, Once laid carefully in a long box he called the Gallery for pick up. While waiting he fixed himself a little something on the electric skillet. A porkchop and fried potatoes cooked slowly as he anticipated their joke.

Martin arrived early and helped the small staff move pieces to give his prominence. The lights on the walls over pictures were dimmed. Sculptures were moved closer to the walls. As the staff put out chairs and tables Martin adjusted the lights for maximum effect. He found a long ladder and dropped a line over a hook in the ceiling then hung a box curtain over his piece, the other end he placed near the podium for the unveiling.

The day of the unveiling was a surprise. Arthur must have used all his pull. The gallery was crowded. The boxed curtain hung over the sculpture. The guests were seated in front of a podium where Arthur stood, and Martin sat. The wine, cheese, crackers, and fruit that graced the side table had rapidly diminished.

Arthur explained about the piece at length and the artist who had created this magnificent work. Martin rose and thanked everyone for coming to the unveiling of his latest work. "The time has come for me to unveil so would everyone please gather at the curtain.

The work was surrounded with people, the lights in the gallery dimmed further. Martin pulled the cord to raise the curtain. The ooohs and ahhs that sounded brought smiles to the duo's faces. Their joke was going to be a huge success. For the next half hour, the sculpture was studied, the dimmer switch repeatedly adjusted, conversation babbled. When the time for bidding arrived, the assembly sat with cards in their laps. The galleries auctioneer stood at the podium and again read the description of the work.

The bidding started at $500.00. A card shot up and the race was off. Arthur murmured to Martin that they might get maybe $4,000.00 at the most but the bidding was swift and rose past that almost immediately. It was into the $7,000.00s when Martin's conscience whacked him.

He stood up interrupting the bidding and walked to the podium. "Ladies and Gentlemen, before things get much farther, I feel the need to explain something. This meeting and exhibit were all part of an elaborate April Fool's joke. The piece is for sale, but I want you to know what you're getting for your money. The "bottle" is simply a burnt-out light bulb. I liked the pattern that had formed naturally and created the base for it as a showcase. If you still wish to bid, we can begin again or if you want, we can continue from where bidding left off. What do you wish to do."

The auctioneer returned to the podium and asked for a show of cards. It was decided that bidding would resume where it had left off. To Martin and Arthur's surprise and delight bidding was now faster than before. When bidding reached $8,000.00 Martin was practically in tears. At the moment he was almost skint. The extra money would serve as a cushion until the next sale.

At $8,500.00 bidding stopped. It had been won by a private collector who had it wrapped up and placed in his van. He was given a certificate of authenticity after handing over cash money. The commission was removed, Martin received $6,200.00. He tried to split the money with Arthur. It was adamantly refused. For a while at least, Martin had enough money to do more than just get by.

Martin was so elated at his good fortune, he treated Arthur to an excellent dinner and champagne. Over dinner Arthur discussed Martins' next project. Martin was fiddling with his mashed potatoes sculpting them into a model of the face he had created days ago and then destroyed. Arthur broke into his reverie with a question. "Martin, not to beat a dead horse, why not set yourself up only doing some of the more avant-garde works? You can work on the serious stuff after you have more money built up."

Martin smashed the potatoes apart and looked down at Arthur. "You really don't know me at all do you." He dropped the fork onto the plate and pushed the rest away. "In all the time we've known each other you still don't get it. I want to be exclusively a classical artist in the mode of Davinci and Michelangelo, I'm not a Picasso or a Duchamp. I want to be taken seriously." Arthur raised an eyebrow, "you know damn well what I mean." He lay back in his chair and rubbed his temples.

Arthur apologized, "I know pal but there's bills to pay and let's face facts, the Avant-garde is what is paying them for you. Do a few more and then you can try your hand at the serious stuff again." Martin paid the bill, rising, he took Arthur by the hand and promised he'd try. He walked out of the restaurant with shoulders bowed and his feet shuffling on the sidewalk. Dragging himself the ten blocks to his studio he contemplated his next artistic endeavor.

Arthur headed to the Califario Art Museum and went with the curator to the archives to sort through some boxes. He was hoping to find something new to write an article about. As an established and respected historian, he had the right of passage to many a museum's enclave. Walking into the rear of the museum they entered the storage area. Here amongst shelves of boxes and flat unframed canvases were items not on display. All were being catalogued and available to be examined. Under bright fluorescent lights he sat at a folding table with an open box marked Charcoal and Chalk.

He examined piece after piece, nothing excited his attention until he came on one that seemed vaguely familiar. The sketch was done in red chalk similar to sketches done by Michelangelo but subtly different enough that it couldn't be his. It couldn't be a Davinci or Raphael either, but it was still damn familiar.

The name Michelangelo kept ringing in his head and wouldn't stop. He examined it closely again, yes, there were similarities to Michelangelo's works but if he was honest, it was more as if someone was copying his style. Perhaps a student or one of his assistants was taking notes and working out a picture of their own. For a moment he was reminded of a sketch by Martin. He studied the sketch under a brighter light.

It was a portrait of a young woman set in a street. Behind her was a church with an ornate clock tower, the time showing 10:10. She was painting a field of flowers with several birds in which only a portion was completed. Beside the painting was a scene of a market with the alley being sketched a darker red than the rest. On the alley entrance were roman numerals XV.VI. MDXLVI. If this was a date it worked out to September 15th, 1546.

He asked permission to take some pictures for analysis which was granted. He used his antique vest pocket Kodak Autograph camera, "an antique to capture an antique," he thought as he snapped away. The curator invited Arthur back to his office for a cup of tea and sandwiches.

Over a light meal the Curator opened his mind to Arthur. "I just wanted to fill you in on the history of that sketch. It was found in a sealed wood case in Michelangelo's home. Most of the sketches were distributed around and we received this along with some others. The odd thing is that while it is very similar to Michelangelo's sketches, especially those accomplished around 1546 we can say for sure it wasn't his.

They chatted for a while more and Arthur again thanking the curator for the information, lunch and the perusal of the box, rose to leave. As he neared the door he turned with a grin, "maybe as they say of some of Shakespeare's plays it was just another artist with the same name." They both laughed and Arthur went back to his apartment to rest. It had been a long day and tomorrow promised to be just as active.

EXPERIMENTATION

Arthur stopped by the studio early bringing breakfast. Over western omelets, toast, and a carafe of coffee they discussed Martin's next artistic endeavor. Arthur opened his mouth to speak but was halted by Martins raised hand "Before you beat me over the head about my doing more new-wave projects, I've decided to take your "advice"." Martin leaned back in his chair and placed a foot on an open desk drawer. "You own the gallery, and you know what sells. So, whatever you suggest for me to create I'll do." He spoke with a tinge of bitterness Arthur couldn't help but recognize.

Arthur stood and paced around the studio. "Martin, you're being unfair, I will put out any piece you want me to but damn it, what's the point of working your heart out on these classical sculptures when hardly anybody wants them. Had you been alive a couple of centuries ago they'd be worth a fortune but not so much today. Your best works are the ones that test your unique imagination. Your combination of sculpture and electronics are your signature pieces. Those are the ones that bring in the critics and bring us both a return. Let's face it, I have to look out for my gallery as well as you so I'm going to push for works that sell."

Martin finished off his cup of coffee. "For my new piece I was thinking of buying a new computer, best I can find. I want to do an open space hologram. With a top-of-the-line computer I won't have to purchase another for a while. I can run a computer decently but don't have a clue about the innards. You keep up on that stuff, would you come with and help me pick one out?" Martin tossed his cup in the trash, stood, and stretched.

Arthur was amenable, "Sure but I need to know what use you're going to put it to. Do you need a good graphics card, plenty of memory or storage space?" They continued the discussion walking to the car and on the way to the computer store. They worked out that what was needed was extra memory and the best co-processor for good measure. With the new computer in hand, they headed back to the studio.

Martin began the process of transferring everything from the old computer onto the new. Arthur was seated on a stool watching over his shoulder. Martin was announcing the programs that were already installed. One intrigued Arthur as he had heard about it in Computer Monthly's newest edition. "Martin, take a look at this." Arthur pointed to the program as it was loading. "I read about this one. They've given you a short-timed sample, the full program costs ten thousand." Martin whistled at the sum,. "What's it do for that kind of dough." An imprint of the Realtime logo appeared on the screen as Arthur activated it. Next screen was blank except for two input sites. One was for date and time, one for location. The note under location requested inputs be as detailed as possible. Apparently, Lat/long was the preferred method of input but it would accept addresses.

Arthur explained as he inputted the location outside the studio. "The main servers are connected to every satellite, camera, and library around the world. It can show any place in real time. He put the date and time in for the present and pressed enter. What was shown on the screen was the outside of the studio looking in through the window. Martin turned around and the image in the window did also. Looking at the screen he waved his hand, the image did as well. "Pretty impressive. Too bad it can't show the past."

Arthur grinned and entered Paris May 2nd, 1869, at 1500. The address was 32 Rue Richer. On the screen showed people walking into the grand opening of the Folies Berger. "It looks like we're actually seeing the real event." Martin dragged up a chair with his foot, sat, staring in wonder at the screen. Arthur hastened to explain. "It uses every available picture and video and any information it can find to build a recreation. From what they say it's as real as it is possible to get, hence the expense. I've got to get back. Have fun with the new toy." Arthur went back to the Gallery to get ready for the next sale.

Intrigued, Martin played with Realtime a little more then decided to work on the hologram. He went to a shelf and found Henison's Book of Electronic Projects. He picked out the chapter that discussed holograms, their construction and uses. He had always been fascinated by the prospects, now he was ready to put theory into practice.

Apparently, what he wanted to create would need mirror tiles, lasers, glass prisms and micro motors all set into a frame. Using the book as a guide he created the frame and installed mirrors and glass light splitters. A quick bus ride to an electronics supply store and he brought home a used helium neon laser. Hooking the laser through his computer he projected a picture into the frames center. What was shown was a flat, ghostly representation of his screen. Nice but not really very interesting. He split the laser beam several more times and projected the same picture at a slightly different angle in each. Now what showed was more solid and seemed to be hovering in the air a little above the base. He added sandbags to the table legs to eliminate any vibrations. Chuckling he realized it was going to work.

From a drawer he gathered the pictures he had once taken of the studio from every angle. Running down to Walgreens he had them placed onto a floppy disk as well as doubles of everything printed out. The disk he loaded into the computer and projected the pictures through the laser beams. He moved mirrors and splitters around so the image could be larger. It stood now as a six-inch square. The details were clear but it retained a flatness that wasn't what he wanted. Still, it was closer to what he had visualized just more in the nature of a detailed flat cube. He poured himself a glass of the Martel and reached for the phone to call Arthur. "Not yet," he thought as he hung it up again "I can do better before I call him".

He shut everything down and inserted all the components onto servos and bars and runners so that the pieces could be raised, lowered, and turned. These he loaded onto a patch board. Now he could reconfigure it easier. For a week he worked adjusting beam by beam and mirror by mirror so that the table was now a mass of posts holding lasers, mirrors, splitters and cards. He cut up the pictures and created a diorama that would be projected above the table. Running this through the computer he heard the fans speed up. He was trying to force the computer into doing the utmost it was capable of. There were other programs running in the background that he required to capture the diorama and shunt it through the laser for dividing, compressing and reconfiguring the image. He crossed his fingers and trusted in luck he wasn't going to test it until Arthur arrived.

Calling Arthur over to see his newest project he went over everything until his arrival. Arthur burst excitedly through the door and beelined towards the table. The sight was just confusing enough that Arthur stood there scratching his head and looking blank. Martin rebooted the computer and ran the images through it. As it loaded, he explained. "The diorama is being viewed through a dual lens like a camera. This goes through the computer for shuffling and reconstruction. Then it's sent through the laser and split up bouncing towards the center."

The program pushed through the image, it slowly rotated slightly above the table. Arthur walked around the projected image of the studio evaluating it critically. "It's interesting to see a hologram without the aid of backing glass. Looks like it could be a good start." For the next hour Martin and Arthur experimented placing different objects in place of the Diorama. Martin tightened the Hologram until it was as "solid" a visual as was possible. Arthur was intrigued. Martin explained the next step.

I want to put the table upright and try and project the image in front. I can even make a pedestal so I can have it rotate images for a whole slew of exhibits. Martin shook his head in wonder at his friend's imagination. It's what made their partnership successful. Martin had the ideas and Arthur could sell them. "I'm sorry I can't stay longer but I've got to head to a meeting. I'll drop by after it's over and see what progress you've made. This may be your top project after all."

Before leaving he assisted to stand the worktable on its end. Martin added a full mirror to the tabletop in order to project the image away from the table and into the open. Resetting the lasers to bounce over the large mirror he was able to create a holographic image hovering freely in space. He walked around it well pleased. With the new computer he could leave the projection running as he checked on a few things.

Opening the Realtime program, he checked on some of the latest favorite locations. He zeroed in on the front of his place again. He liked seeing the frontage from the outside view. His fingers fumbled on the keyboard and the screen image was projected where the hologram had been. Martin walked over to see the street and door of his studio projected in front of him. He laughed at the perfection of the image. It was so real he felt he could reach through and open the door. Laughing at the silliness he tried it.

He walked around to the "front" of the image. Once there he stepped forward cautiously and stepped onto the sidewalk. He was suddenly outside the studio. It took a moment to realize what had just happened and his blood ran cold. Grasping the doorknob, he turned and opened the door. The studio he walked into was his own. There could be no doubt about it. The doorway was still projected in the center of the studio but now it showed open. He walked through it again and again each time was the same. He placed objects differently and they showed in the places he had placed them every time. This was real. Somehow with the two programs combined he had created a doorway or a portal. His face flushed with excitement. His enthusiasm evaporated quickly when he saw a countdown clock in the right top corner. It showed 10 minutes of the sample's runtime left. Immediately shutting it down he paused for thought. As he brewed a cup of coffee, he considered the possibilities.

If he wanted to experiment with this program more, he was going to have to purchase the full thing. Checking his bank balance, he figured he'd need about four thousand dollars. He lay down on the cot and considered what he could do with the current setup that would procure him the necessary funds. He shivered at the decision that crystalized. Against all his principles he was going to have to steal the money. This was too important to delay it even for the sake of his conscience.

Martin sat up and rubbed his temples. He had made his decision and fully intended to carry it out, but that didn't mean he liked it. The clock on the wall registered 0630. He locked the studio door and drew the curtains across the window. Turning on the computer, he ran a test using GPS coordinates instead of an address. He entered coordinates inside the studio. The portal was now inside with dimensions of 6 feet tall and a foot and a half wide. He walked through, turned and walked back. It could be used as sort of a temporal doorway. Every test that worked meant that despite his misgivings it could be done.

His heart was racing as he realized the plan would work. He shut the program off with 8 minutes remaining. He needed the coordinates for a place with money. There was a bank close, but he needed to know the exact location of the vault since he couldn't spend time trying to figure out a combination, he wanted to walk straight into it. He'd have to wait until tomorrow, then after a brief visit to the bank he could set his plan in motion. He went out back into the alley for a smoke.

Outside he lit a Marlborough and inhaled deeply. The cigarette calmed him down nicely. He sat on the stoop, leaning back against the cement wall and slowly let out a plume of smoke. He pictured stacks of bills piled on his desk. He heard the kaching of the doorbell and took another drag. From inside he heard Arthur come in calling out for him. He answered sedately, the smoke mingling with his words. "Be in in a sec, I'm outside smoking." Leisurely finishing the last few puffs, he ground out the cig and walked inside.

He barely saw Arthur seated at the computer. Seeing was difficult since Arthur was using the predawn light from the window as his only illumination. As Martin came in through the back door to the desk, he saw the Realtime program was running. The Eiffel tower was lit up on the screen resplendent in multicolored lights. The view was impressive. Martin joined in admiration of the view as well, until he agitatedly noticed the top right-hand corner read 3:27. With a gasp he lunged forward and pulled the plug, much to Arthur's irritation.

"What gives?" He questioned querulously. Martin steadied himself. "Sorry but there was only a couple of minutes left and I need those minutes for an experiment later today." He worked to get his heart rate lower and his voice under control. "What brings you round this early in the morning?"

Arthur held out his cell and showed a message from the Floor Manager of the Gallery, "Martin's piece was a considerable success and the writeup has stirred interest in more of his works. If you find another piece or can induce him into producing, we can guarantee another large audience for the sale next month."

Martin sauntered over to the shelf and pulled out a sculpture of a head he had cast a while ago. Placing it into a wooden box, he strategically drilled holes according to his notes and placed winking Christmas lights in all the holes. Once plugged in he set the timer to slow. The face had thin wedges of plastic that cast shadows changing the face considerably. The intermittent lights changed the face in a continual flow of light and shadows. Arthur watched in awe as the face became mobile, it practically came to life. He thumped Martin on the back. "Pal you're finally beginning to hit your stride. This should net quite another thousand at the very least. Come next month, you should be set again. With what you have now you can afford to sit back and wait while you improve on this hologram piece. I think better things are coming for us both!"

Martin packed up the case and added twine and a handle so Arthur could take it away. Arthur leaned against a shelf as he waited. "I'll take some pictures and do a writeup on it for next week." He grabbed the handle and shuffled out the door burdened by the weight of the sculpture. He looked back and saw Martin was looking dejected again. Modern art was all well and good, it paid the bills, but he also understood that Martin's dream was to create classical sculptures. He felt for him, but he had an obligation to the gallery and himself too and this stuff sold.

Alone again, Martin looked at the clock. 0830 and the bank would be open at 10:00. He went out for breakfast and then went back home to change. Setting his cell phone to video record he placed it in his breast pocket. As casually as his excitable nature would allow him, he strolled around the bank recording from every angle he could. He had to time things so that he could record what he needed but not stay so long as to excite suspicion.

Figuring he'd need to ask something not readily available, he went to the teller and asked for thirty rolls of Susan B

Anthony dollars. The teller looked up questioningly. He explained it was for a mural he was creating. The teller brought the request to the attention of a guard who opened the vault so she could retrieve his rolls. The inside was spacious. He could see bags of coins and wrapped bills lining the shelves. Plenty of room to walk and turn about in there. He took his bag of coins and heaved them onto his shoulder.

Returning, he staggered into the studio weighed down with seven hundred and fifty dollars in coins. He dumped them into a desk drawer. Connecting his phone to the computer he viewed the location of the safe and using google maps zeroed in on the center of it. Marking down the coordinates, he next worked out an estimate of the best collection process and the time needed. To gather the money would take moments as long as he didn't get distracted. He could be in and out in a couple of minutes. This gave him a minute and a half grace.

He pulled out a pair of cotton gloves, a pair of coveralls, some shoe covers and a flashlight. Laying these on the cot under the blanket he worked out his plans. As he saw it, he could wait and see if the auction could procure the funds he needed or he could continue his current plan. Patience unfortunately, not being his strong suit, he decided on the latter. The more he thought about the risk and consequences, the more he was still trying to dissuade himself. However, by nightfall he had regained his determination to see it through.

He set a timer on his phone and another on the computer. He turned the computer screen so it faced the portal. Once through it would provide a modicum of light since he couldn't risk the lights from the studio being on. The flashlight would provide quick focus.

He grabbed an old plastic shopping bag from a drawer and donned his outfit. He loaded the program, activated the timers, then inputted the coordinates. The portal formed and showed nothing but inky darkness. Stepping through he looked back to see the screen counting down. His flashlight batteries were weak, the light barely illuminated. He swept the shelves, his breath coming in gasps as he noticed that the stacks were in no particular order. He would have to waste time in searching and time was a luxury he didn't have. He silently cursed the slovenly way this bank worked and determined to take his business elsewhere. His flashlight spluttered and went out. The only light emanated from the studio through the portal.

Soon he was blindly filling his plastic bag with what he hoped were the choicest morsels. A stack here a stack from there, he grabbed at random hoping he would gather the amount he needed. He didn't have time to check. His phone was set to beep when he had thirty seconds left. Surprised that the phone hadn't beeped yet he checked and saw the phone battery had died. He heard the click of tumblers; someone was opening the vault. He had seconds to make his escape. Leaping to return home his bag split and stacks fell as he flew into the studio just as the timer hit zero and the portal closed. For all his effort he noticed he had gained only one stack of tens. His attempt at robbery had only gained him one thousand dollars and he couldn't go back for the rest. He slammed the stack into the desk with the coins. He had sacrificed his honor and integrity for nothing. Kicking the drawer closed he went to bed.

In the morning Martin put in a frustrated call to Arthur to see if he could speed up the auction. Shocked, Arthur tried to dissuade his impetuous friend. "Pal, the longer we wait the greater the chance for a full group to bid!" Martin was not swayed and requested the auction be held within the next three days at the latest or he would withdraw his piece. Arthur had only just put in the writeup, interest wouldn't be peaked for at least a week. He tried in vain to change Martins' mind. Beaten yet unwilling to withdraw the piece, Arthur arranged for the show in three days. However, to allow for the greatest amount of time he placed the auction at night.

Irritated at his friend's obstinacy Arthur pounded the keys of his typewriter as he changed the date for the auction. He ripped the page out and slapped it in the box for transmittals. He lit a cigarette and thought about Martins change of plans. What he was doing made no sense and he felt it was necessary to find out why the rush. Arriving outside the studio he peered in the window. Martin was despondently working on his holographic projection setup. He had created another shadow head and placed it into a larger box with more lights. The holographic head that hovered in front of the mirror looked as though they were conversing. Opening the door slowly so as not to disturb Martin, he saw his friend seated on a stool having a conversation with the image. Somehow, he had hooked an Alexa through the system. It was speaking out of the image, the mouth moving in unison with the words.

The head was reporting local news and was describing a robbery that had the police baffled. Sometime in the night someone had broken into the bank, opened the vault and made off with a thousand dollars in small bills. Some bundles of much higher denominations were found strewn over the floor. The vault was relocked, the robber had somehow left without setting off the alarms. The nightwatchman had supposedly surprised the robbers but how they had made their escape was a mystery There were no fingerprints or shoe prints to aid the police and they had placed the matter on hold pending further investigation.

Arthur stood leaning against a shelf and wondered why Martin seemed to suddenly relax. He placed a hand on Martin's shoulder which made him jump, screech and whip around putting his hands placatingly in the air. At the sight of his friend, he relaxed once more. Arthur put an arm around his shoulder and took him outside for a smoke. He lit his own then lit Martin's off it. Beginning the conversation with small talk about his latest article, the price of marble and the newest oil paints from Mars and Markaham, he noticed his friend was still tense. He changed tact. "Pal, I think you've been working too hard. Let's go to the pub and grab a beer and burger." Martin inhaled the rest of his cigarette and ground out the end. "O.k. Let me turn everything off and lock up."

In the dark of the bar the two men sat quietly. The only conversation had been regarding the order and that was reduced to two words, Beer, Burger. Arthur figured it was up to him to get the ball rolling. "Pal, what's the rush on the sale, you still should have plenty of cash left from the last one, so why the rush?"

Martin lay back in his seat and closed his eyes. He knew this conversation was imminent but hadn't expected this onslaught so quick. He straightened up and slicked back his hair. Leaning on the table he decided to offer an explanation. "I think I've made a breakthrough. "I need the program working though to make it a reality" He edged closer to Arthur I think I've created a way to move through space and possibly time.

Arthur's mouth hung open, the partially chewed food sliding off his tongue and slowly landing in his lap. Martin closed Arthur's mouth and tossed him his napkin. Arthur wiped up the mess and stared at Martin. "This isn't a whisky dream like you had about a pair of tweezers and the buffalo once, is it?" Martin pulled out his phone and showed the recording he had made when he had twice brought the portal into the lab. Arthur studied the video, it looked real but, no it couldn't be, no buts, it was real. He turned astonished eyes to Martins smiling face.

Martin took back his phone and locked the screen. "I haven't told anyone about this except you and I don't intend to. Eat up and we'll go back to the lab." Arthur waved over the waiter and asked for the check, suddenly he wasn't hungry anymore.

Arthur sat and smoked with rapid puffs coming from the glowing end of his cigarette. Martin set up the old computer. Loading up Realtime, he shunted it through his laser setup. By using his old computer, he had the sample again, at least for as long as the computer lasted. It was low on minutes by now after the tests he had already done but was still usable to prove what he had said. He knew he was about to fry it even with a couple of fans added but it was necessary for Arthur to see it, "O.k. I'm going to program the studio from outside and you'll see I can walk through. Doing so the door of the studio was projected. Arthur stepped onto the projected sidewalk and vanished from inside and reappeared outside. He reached for the door and could see himself in the projection. The door opened and he walked inside. Arthur watched and tried to wrap his mind around what he was seeing.

The portal disappeared in a plume of smoke as the computer caught fire and burst into flames. Martin shuddered at the thought he could have been within the portal when it caught on fire. Arthur grabbed the blanket from the cot as Martin opened the back door. The gust of wind passing through the studio and out the still opened front door fanned the flames to greater intensity. They tossed the blanket over the computer and lifting the table it rested on they carried it out back. Hurling the table and computer they kicked sand and gravel until the fire was out.

In the studio Martin looked over the damage. Not bad all things considered. He went to close the front door and noticed slight scorch marks on the edge where the projection had been closest to the fire. Had he been within the portal then assuredly he would have gone up too. Arthur came in and turned on the other computer. He had an inkling that with Martins setup there were more possibilities than just a quick way to go outside. Something like this could transport you anywhere in a moment. Hell, there was even the possibility it could send you through time since the Realtime program could bring up a facsimile. He was quick to realize the possibilities open to both of them. Without Martin's knowledge he accessed the Realtime site, entered his information and bought the full program. He shut down the computer and informed Martin that he would set the auction up as soon as possible. "In the meantime, you might want to check Realtime again. I think something reset and the program is working again. He left in a hurry to get to the Gallery.

Martin started up the computer to see what Arthur meant. He looked at the right-hand corner and the timer was gone. A bugle sounded and a flashing notification congratulated him on owning the full version. Martin flopped into his chair with tears streaming down. He opened the side drawer to get tissues, the bundles of bills smote his conscience. He set the portal to the vault once more and returned the bills. He was tempted to add a sincere apology but felt it was better to be safe and remain anonymous. Now with the full program open to him he contemplated his next move. He surmised that he had access to anywhere in seconds and quite possibly anywhen. His only problem was that whatever choice he made; the portal would have to remain open. Surely, he thought, he could think of some way to surmount that difficulty.

A TRIP IN THE PRESENT

The sky darkened giving everything in view a greenish hue. Martin stepped outside in eager anticipation of the coming storm. When the world began to go green it wouldn't be long before all hell broke loose. In excited anticipation he noted every change. The wind started blowing, the sky grew darker until it was black as pitch. There was a flash of lightning and the crackle and blast of thunder. The window of his studio rattled from the onslaught. The clouds opened and buckets of water poured from the sky. Martin shivered with excitement, also from the fact that he was drenched. These were the types of storms that fired his imagination bringing inspiration with every flash of lightning or crash of thunder.

Inside he turned on the gas heater to dry off and brewed a fresh pot of coffee. He thought about what he could do regarding the problem of an open portal. He had an artistic mentality which could just supply a simple answer. Create an overlay that would camouflage the portal. He turned on the computer and accessed Realtime. Since he could travel, he decided to do a trip to somewhere familiar. He started inputting an area he had visited in his youth. It was set for a little place in Italy right off the market on Strada di campo di Fiori. There was a church with an intricate clock tower that had fascinated him. If he set the portal inside the alleyway to the left of the church, the dark would take care of most of the problem. An overlay with a black cloth projected over one mirror would combine with the portal and would take care of the rest. From a shelf he brought out some black felt and hung it over the mirror. He programed for present day, put in a call to his bank that he'd be in Italy for the day and walked through.

In the darkness of the alley, he looked towards the street twenty yards away. He saw a light, glaringly bright in front of the archway. From behind him came rumble then a flash of light from the edges of the portal's cover. Rushing back, he hit a wall instead of a portal. Kicking at the wall and banging it with his fists he cursed himself for a fool. "Damn it," He thought as he walked towards the street, "I never think two steps ahead. He walked and realized he hadn't taken a passport or any papers. "I wonder if I can get a plane ticket without a passport. Well, if nothing else I can put a call in to Arthur." Only slightly reassured he found a phonebooth and asked to be connected to the American Consulate. He made an appointment for 1600, checked his watch and found he had plenty of time to look around.

Entering the street, he was swept along with a mass of humanity. As he passed a bank he got some cash from an ATM. If he was going to be trapped here a while, he felt it was only right to enjoy it a bit. Dislocating himself from the stream of people, he wandered around the market stalls. For a moment he stopped to admire the view. On both sides of the street old brick buildings with iron fenced balconies framed the sides while at ground level stalls of flowers, fruits, bread and anything you might desire were hawked in a mass chorus of voices. He purchased some chestnuts expertly split and warm to munch on as he meandered.

Under a canopy to his right were boxes of spices, pungent and fragrant, that sent his gastric juices surging. Next on both sides were many varieties of fish brought in daily from the nearby Ionian Sea. A wedge of cheese, olives, bread and wine were gathered next, He purchased a basket to hold his feast then hurried back to where he had begun.

Seated on the edge of a fountain he relaxed and enjoyed his repast. From across the street, he saw the clock of the tower register 1145. He would wait to hear the bells toll then he would have to consider the predicament of getting home. On the cuff of his shirt, he wrote a reminder to always leave a message for Arthur about where and when he was going as well as packing a bag with passport and cell phone and anything else he might need for emergencies. As he waited on the bells, he watched a young lady of about twenty-five set up an easel and open a box of paints.

The easel had seen much use, yet she extended its legs with ease showing that though old it was kept in good repair. He watched as she brought out a thin square of wood and began to set colors on her pallet. Martin admired the smooth brushwork as she moved the paint in graceful sweeps. Her lines were blurred depicting the rush of people while the buildings and stalls were clear and defined. He congratulated her on her painting.

She acknowledged his compliment with her best smile. Her chestnut hair shone as she placed it over her shoulder. "Thanks, it's only a hobby but I *love* painting, after a hard day at the hospital it's a great way to relax." As she painted, she got that introverted stare of a person immersed in their work. Martin brought out a pencil and picked up a sheet of brown paper trapped by the wind against the fountain. Laying it on his leg proceeded to sketch her.

In his sketch he captured the luster of her thick hair, the furrow of her brow and the small upturn to her nose. Her lips pressed together in a small line when she was concentrating. He made smooth graceful lines as he drew the billowing flowered blouse. Beside her he sketched in a small martin on a branch nearby. He kept her in sharp relief and lightly penciled the street, market, church and alley. He was shading in the alley, when he noticed flashes of light emanating from within the tunnel. His curiosity rising, he dropped the sketch into her box of paints. With halting strides to avoid the contrary flow of people he peered into the alley. A piercing yell of "Martin" rebounded off the bricks like an echo chamber.

Relief flowing through him at the sound of Arthur's voice and the sight of the open portal he barreled into his studio. Arthur closed the portal and enthusiastically hugged Martin. In his relief at being home he returned the hug and kissed Arthur on the top of his balding head. Over a glass of Jamerson, Arthur told how he had discovered Martin missing and discovered his whereabouts.

"When I dropped by to see you and make sure you were o.k. I saw the lights out and figured the fuse had blown. It sure had; the fuse looked as if you could have done another sculpture like the bulb. I was relieved the computer and all your paraphernalia were safe. What did surprise me was I couldn't find you. I couldn't believe even you would be out in that hell of a storm." Martin nodded in agreement.

Arthur refilled his glass and continued, "I looked around for a note or something, then I saw some numbers scratched on the desk near the computer and figured by the dots they were coordinates. Loading up the computer it went right back to what it was doing when the power went off. The portal was active but just black. I couldn't figure out what the hell you were doing or where I had opened it to. I tossed a pebble through to makes sure it was as safe as you made out it was. Then looking through the portal I saw into the alley, the street and across to the fountain with you drawing and a dear young thing painting. I shone the light which somehow you noticed thank goodness, and came running over. Pal, I am damn glad to see you!"

Martin drained the last drop from his glass and went to the bathroom to rinse it out. "I'm glad to see you too. I'm sorry, I should have left a note of what I was doing. I'll try and remember that next time. Think about it though. I stepped from here over to Italy with no problem!" At Arthurs raised brows he amended his comment. "O.k. some problems did arise once there, but getting there was a snap." He put his feet on the desk and pulled a sketch pad. He did a quick rendering of the young lady at work at the hospital and painting.

Martin suddenly had an epiphany. He went over to the computer and did an overlay for the borough of Mildenhall in England. For years he had spent thousands of dollars having things shipped. Now he was going to go in person and just carry a few bags home. Lot's cheaper and he could pick and choose. Finding a secluded area in a closed off section of the car park of a Tescos he opened the portal and went shopping. Before he left, he emphasized to Martin several times not to close the portal.

Martin finished his sketch. Through the portal he watched Arthur as he walked into Tescos. It amused him that Arthur was so excited he was practically skipping. He sat down and started working out trips they could take together or individually. One thing he needed was a way to get home. He sketched out possible ways to create a portable portal. He needed another laptop and a way to conceal it, a carriable something to act as the portal and conceal the works. By the time Arthur was back with his treasures Martin had a pretty good idea for a second trip and the means to return.

Martin followed Arthur out to his car and requested they go to the computer store again. He explained what he wanted to build and why. Arthur shrugged and opened the door. As they sped off Martin lay back in the leather seat working out how to combine everything into a paintbox and easel.

On the way back to the studio they stopped at a painting supply store for a commodious painter's box. In the studio Martin inserted the laptop into base of the paint box. He grinned as he pasted slits of wood around the sides to hold a partitioned box for his paints and brushes. Arthur was busy constructing a frame for an easel. It was going to be too heavy and cumbersome to be carried around so they determined to find a place to rent wherever and whenever they went so it could be set up and left. As they worked out the recesses for holding the mirrors, glass and lasers it occurred to Arthur that for any time before 1945 they couldn't use it, no electricity. Martin wasn't so sure.

Martin brought out a set of clay pots. Each had a couple of posts in the center and these were held in place with a cork stopper. From a cardboard box he brought out a plastic bag filled with clear liquid. "It's battery acid although vinegar can work just as well in an emergency." He explained as he filled the pots. He linked them together then added a socket. Plugging in the laptop showed that it was charging. Arthur was only slightly reassured. "Alright, that works pretty good but aren't you going to have to keep refilling the pots?"

Martin shook his head and went to the shelves of odds and ends he used as fill for paintings. He pulled a cage with a stuffed bird in it. The base was two inches thick and covered in wire mesh. Removing the bottom, he began constructing a power supplier. A fan blade hovered above alternating magnets. The post went into a mini generator similar to one used to work a bicycle light. At the speed it spun in the slightest breeze it would take three hours to recharge the pots. If he kept the generator hooked up to the pots the depletion rate was low enough he could operate at minimum power for quite a while. For the rest of the day they tested the portable portal setup. Starting off with local areas such as forests and caves they then tried places all over the world. Bangkok Thailand, Navarre France, Wiesbaden Germany, the Fiji Islands, Mudgee Australia, and the top of Mount Rainier.

Now with the tests accomplished they discussed a possible trip through time. Arthur wasn't sure if it would work or not. After all what was shown in Realtime was a simulation, an approximation of what should be. Would they really be able to travel in time. For an answer they looked up when all the satellites and cameras weren't around. They decided to test it in the 1950's. Martin and Arthur found something that was the same in both times. One of the few buildings still exactly the same was called the St Vernon Chapel.

Both men had visited it in their youth. "Remember sitting in the stalls up by the roof?" Martin asked. Arthur smiled and reminisced. "Sure, there was a little hole in the wall that I used to stuff my green army men in. I don't think I ever collected them all." Martin programmed the portal for the 1950's and tried to fix it so they would emerge in the loft. The portal opened and Arthur tossed a penny through as a test then walked quietly through himself. He found the hole and using a pen, he dug out three small plastic army men. He marked one with the pen and replaced it. Back in the studio they drove down to the church and climbed the steps up to the loft. Arthur arrived at where the hole should have been. "Looks like it's been filled, now we'll never know."

Martin was desperate and carefully made a slit beneath the molding. Pulling slightly at the plaster in spite of Arthurs remonstrations he dug out a small soldier with his initials and the current date. A grumble behind them and both men saw a priest with a stern expression glaring at them. He departed leaving the men shaken and apprehensive. He came back shortly with a can of plaster and a spatula. Handing them over he departed. Martin took the task on himself and carefully filled the hole again. Shamefaced they departed running to the car like two kids making a hasty escape.

"Well, it worked." Martin was tossing and catching the army man and grinning. Arthur was suddenly worried. "Martin, I'm not so sure about this. We've got something here that's way out of our league. We don't know what could happen to the present if we go back in time." Martin dropped the piece of plastic. "Damn it, I want to use it. As long as I don't kill anyone or do something drastic it'll be fine. I just want to meet a few artists, see some sights and maybe eat out a bit." Arthur wasn't convinced and they talked as day turned to night." Sitting in the pub later over several beers, they had almost reached an agreement. Martin was writing down what he called the rules of engagement.

1. Only you and I can know about this (for now).

2. Can't kill anyone no matter how tempted. If the need to fight arises get them so they can't do you any harm, then walk away.

3. We alternate trips with the other watching at all times.

4. No falling in love, we can't bring someone out of their time.

5. No stealing or trying to make ourselves rich through time manipulation. It might draw too much attention or end the world as we know it.

Arthur had earlier suggested that they possibly try and change things, but this would surly mean life or death for lots of people if they tried. It would require a lot more thought if they ever considered it seriously.

Martin wanted to meet the true genius, his hero, Michelangelo. He insisted that with a portal available at both ends it could be done now. Arthur agreed since he could keep an eye on him from the computer screen. He insisted that they do a test to ensure he could track Martin before closing the portal down. Martin wanted to jump right in but Arthur, being a bit more levelheaded, explained that if he couldn't track and something went wrong with the other portal Martin would be up the creek without a paddle.

Martin agreed and set about readying himself for the trip. He went to a nearby jewelry store and purchased some jewels. It was his conjecture that it would be easier to convert jewels than try and find money from the 1600's to take back with him. Arthur would be on standby until Martin gained some funds, selected a suitable establishment, and opened a portal from his end to ensure it was possible. If Martin lost track of Arthur and no word was heard in three days Arthur would begin a series of portal openings where he had let Martin off at. These would be opened at one-hour intervals for only a few seconds unless the site was secluded enough to create a blind. Arthur hurried off to the library to find a map they could use to pinpoint the drop off location.

He returned with a list of probable entry sites. His enthusiasm was beginning to match Martins. He was intrigued at the idea of Martin meeting what he considered one of the greatest masters and set the computer for 1655 Italy. Even more intriguing was if his portal worked as well there as here then Martin could join in the trip. There was plenty to interest a learned Art History enthusiast as well as a gallery owner! He was beginning to think of advantages to himself. They huddled together peering into the computer screen and used the joystick to wander around visiting the sites Arthur had located and seeing which promised the best entre'.

Martin pointed at the monitor, "I think we'll be best at the Piazza di Corcci, it's only a short walk to Michelangelo's home from there. I see a small corner of the alley that we can use. When I go through follow me with the miniport so I can link up when I get a place. Martin locked the screen in a darkened corner of the alley. Rushing to the bathroom he dressed into an outfit he wore to renaissance festivals. He projected the portal, loaded everything onto a wooden cart and waived to Arthur as he walked through. Arthur watched Martin heading off into the distance. He'd have to wait to see if Martin would make contact on his own in the meantime he would follow at a discrete distance.

While Martin faded into the distance, Arthur felt a buzz in his pocket. He checked the messages on his phone. One immediately caught his attention. "The storm caused a leak in the gallery roof. We noticed water dripping down and have removed the paintings to a new location, more items will need to go into storage. We're getting humidity in the second level storage we think will damage more pieces. Sir, we need you here fast so we can get things moved and repairs arranged." He placed a call to the gallery and things were as urgent as the message had made him believe. He figured Martin was well on his way and able to shift for himself for a bit. Dashing off a note should Martin return and not find him, he locked the studio up and peeled off back to the gallery.

Martin was wandering around looking for a jewelers or hock shop. He located the jewelers first and after selling a few baubles he had enough to keep him going for a while. The jeweler was also kind enough to direct him to an apartment with rooms to let. He had contemplated the idea of going to an inn but realized that it would be difficult to ensure the room would be exclusive. Lots of hotels and inns of this time could sell three to a bed. Not an idea that appealed to him.

At the apartment he was given a room on the second floor. Looking it over he agreed to the price asked since it was available to be let for several months. It had a very small kitchen and a privy. They gave him the keys and assisted to help bring in his carted belongings. Locking the door he looked around his new temporary home. Not much, just a bed, a desk, and a chest. The stove had several utensils and pans above it or he could go to the various inns and pubs nearby. He would have to purchase more clothes later but today was just a test. He linked the pot batteries and installed the generator near the window. Setting up the easel he opened the recesses and released mirrors, splitters and glasses. He drew a mylar screen down the back for the mirror and plugged it into the laptop.

Assembly was a breeze after all the practice runs. He was ready in no time. He dragged over a chair and placed the paint box into the hanger to the side of the easel. Taking out the paints he opened up the laptop and fired it up. He loaded up Realtime and as it went through startup, he placed the laser on hold. Rubbing his hands he loaded in coordinates, date and time for his studio. The system seemed to freeze. He rebooted the computer and tried again. Once more the system froze. Scratching his head, he checked the setup again. Everything was set up as it had been in the studio. He rebooted again and waited. He tried a few simple programs they worked just fine. He reloaded up Realtime and entered his studio. He was punching the keys harder than he needed to in his frustration. The system locked up once again. His eyes roved over the screen. They passed the lower right-hand corner. Only then did he notice the small globe with the notification, "NO INTERNET ACCESS".

With no internet, Realtime would run but couldn't connect. He waived in the air hoping to catch Arthur's attention and pointed to the portal trying to intimate that he should open his. For half an hour he continued gesticulating. When nothing happened, he slumped in his chair. He'd have to wait for three days. He only hoped Arthur would be in the studio to turn on the portal.

BACK TO THE GALLERY

Arthur surveyed the damage. The items in the loft were temporarily brought up here when special exhibits were being displayed. He separated each piece by damaged and undamaged. A full third of the stored pieces were damaged and would take a long time for repairs if they were repairable at all. In any case they would lose a great deal of their value. Marta the Floor Managers in charge of moving pieces came quietly up the stairs. She feared that she was about to be fired at best and possibly sued for the damaged pieces. Tripping over the last stair she sprawled on the floor banging into Arthur's leg. He spun around and Marta jumped to her feet apologizing profusely.

"Easy Marta, let's move the good pieces to another spot and start doing the paperwork on the ones we'll have to claim on insurance." Marta rushed to open the basement and unlocked storage bin 6. She heartily wished she had stored all the pieces there in the first place, but Arthur had always told them to use the loft for temporary storage under three days. When they had stored what they could Marta wanted to assist doing the paperwork for the insurance. Arthur assured her he was capable of doing the paperwork alone and ushered her out locking the door behind her,

Seated on an upside-down trash can he set about valuing the losses. As he filled out the information on piece after piece, he was getting more and more frustrated. Try as he might he could only put the values as an estimation of probable selling price based on previous sales of similar pieces. No matter how he tried to fudge the numbers it wasn't going to cover the losses much less make a good profit. His insurance company valuations were always conservative, especially on newer artists. Marta knocked and apologized again through the closed door. As she crept down the stairs, he heard her bemoaning that she hadn't thought about moving the pieces to the basement. "Yeah, me too," thought Arthur as he erased an exorbitant valuation for the painting before him.

The paper ripped as a sudden though struck home like a bolt of lightning. As if in a daze he left the loft. Locking the door he admonished everyone to stay out of it. He went to the basement and opened the storage units and found one which would hold what was ruined. Only it wouldn't be ruined when he put it in there. He grinned as thoughts rushed through his brain. There were possibilities to Martin's invention that he hadn't considered before. First things first though. He had a salvage job to do.

Arriving at the studio he set the program for the outside of the gallery and using a joystick he maneuvered the portal into the loft on the day before the storm. He was almost caught by Marta who had just brought up the last piece and was closing and locking the door. Working quietly and quickly he removed the pieces destined to be damaged and brought them into the studio. Resetting the program, he dropped down into the basement storage to secure the pieces. Dusting off his hands he went back to the gallery. Entering, he saw things were the same as before. He had expected something to be different. Marta approached with none of her previous diffidence. She escorted him to the loft and showed him that the pieces were undamaged. Some pieces were missing though, she had been worried but had found them safe in a storage locker in the basement.

"I don't know how they got there. I didn't move them and nobody else remembers doing it either." She looked up at Arthur with a puzzled and slightly worried expression. Arthur smiled and reassured her that he had done it himself when the storm had started. He claimed he had come in the back entrance and done it so as not to bother the staff. "You all must have been huddled by the front window watching the show." She admitted that such was the case and left to carry on setting up the next exhibits.

In his office Arthur contemplated the advantage of having a time machine at his disposal. With a little effort he was able to save himself many thousands of dollars and turn despair into joy. He went to the restroom and rinsed out his cup to fill it with fresh coffee. Some splashed over the side washing over the portrait of Van Gogh printed on the side. Cleaning the spill off with his sleeve he sat at his desk. He picked up the open magazine he had been reading the day before. He was reading an article that listed Van Gogh's lost works and their current values if ever found. The figures were staggering.

Leaning back and resting he imagined finding one and auctioning it at Sotheby's. The money would allow him to expand and be able to lure better artists to his establishment. Much as he liked his friend, Martin was one of those artists who had to be cozened into producing the works that sold. Left to himself he would go on producing classical sculptures forever and never making much money. Arthur had always been able to convince him to create the sculptures that not only sold easily but brought in larger sums of money. Out of all the artists that were associated with the gallery Martin's work was considered the best and sold regularly. The rest were an average lot whose works sold occasionally but he could not have lived on the commissions.

Arthur's fingers had been tapping on the portion of the article relating details of when Van Gogh was in Hague in 1881. He considered going to visit Van Gogh and securing one of the lost paintings. What a coup it would be. He would be famous and rich. If only there was a way to make his dreams come true. His face flushed as he realized that his dreams could come true after all. Almost giddy with delight he tore his coat off the hook and put it on as he ran down the stairs. He leapt over the door of his car through the open roof and landed in the seat. Ignition on, the motor roared into life and he sped away in a squeal of spinning tires and a spray of flying gravel.

At the studio he checked to see if Martin had returned. No sign yet so he was probably getting acquainted with his new surroundings. He'd check back later and see if Martin was back then, if not he'd have to do a check at the three-day point. It didn't matter if he did it early or later since in this case time was relevant or was that irrelevant. Considering himself free to use the setup for a few hours, He patched in Hague of 1881 into Realtime. On a split screen he pulled up a sketch Van Gogh had done from the window where he was living, he found some items he could look for as landmarks. A long blue roofed building near a large building with a cupola, a tree lined lane fenced about halfway with rectangle fields. It wasn't a lot to go by, but he scanned over the area. It took twenty minutes of searching but he found the blue roofed building and the domed one nearby.

Passing the view down and to the right he didn't see the fields. He looked again at the painting and reversed to the left. A small group of buildings were in front of the fields. If he did this trip, he would have to leave the portal open, He couldn't take a chance on anything going wrong. He checked the weather, circuit breakers, computer, and anything else he could think of. All secure as far as he could tell. He positioned the portal into a shed and opened it into pitch blackness. As he was about to pass through, he remembered the cloth trick Martin had used to disguise the open portal and placed a cloth over one of the mirrors. The result when he passed through was sufficient. He reached through back into the studio. Reassured, he cautiously peeped out of the shed and stepped into a wooded area. Locking the shed as best he could he walked a wide area before emerging onto the lane in front.

From the doorway he looked across the lane to see what was shown in the painting except now it was real life. His heart was racing as he reached up and knocked on the door. He was surprised to find it opened by an elderly woman with a young boy clutching at her leg. He spoke in English then corrected to Dutch. "Excuse me, is Mr. Van Gogh at home?" She ushered him inside as the boy ran off to tell his mother that company had arrived. The cottage was small and though not untidy, was crowded. There were two beds at either corner in the rear, a small cooking range where a pot of soup was simmering and sending off fragment odors of meat and vegetables, A table laid for lunch with a wine bottle centered and covered with a cloth. To the right and front in the illumination of two large windows were a couple of chairs and a small table.

The mother of the small boy was sewing an eye onto a stuffed doll. She half rose as Arthur approached then resumed her sewing. The elderly lady seated Arthur in the empty chair and brought him a glass of wine. Seated and sipping his wine he waited. As unobtrusively as he could he studied the lady. She must have been around forty. Her skin was still taught but was starting to slacken about the neck and arms. Her brown hair was wrapped in cloth and tied up as a cap. Brown eye were focused intently on the work she was performing, and her slender hands moved with graceful ease. Her figure appeared slim but sturdy. Her face at rest was plain but attractive. She tied off the thread, handed the toy to the boy then turned to face Arthur.

He was anxious to hear her voice. She gazed at him steadily for a moment and then her face became warm and welcoming. Her voice though deeper than he expected was also pleasant. She remembered that he had not come to see her, "Vincent is not at home, but he is expected momentarily. He has been spending time with a monsieur Anton Mauve with whom he may be staying a while studying and working on his paintings. My name by the way is Sien,". She held out her hand. Arthur took it not sure whether to kiss it or shake it. He bent over it and then seated himself and made polite talk. She suddenly changed from Dutch to English much to Arthur's surprise. She clapped and laughed at the look on Arthur's face when she switched languages. "Vincent has taught me the languages he knows. It helps to be able to speak sometimes how no one can understand. They spoke on painting, of which she understood little, and on literature which she was very conversant in.

A knock on the door and the elderly lady put aside her knitting and answered it, the young boy flying to beat her there. When the door opened a squeal of delight rang out and the boy could be heard jumping up and down. Vincent Van Gogh entered with the boy pulling at his arm and leading him to his mother. Vincent had no eyes for anyone but Sien who rose and kissed him. When they parted, she introduced him to Arthur stating that he had been waiting for 'the great artist" to return.

Vincent sat opposite Arthur and for a moment the two men looked at each other critically. Arthur finally broke the silence explaining that he had heard of the up-and-coming artist and was curious to know if he could purchase one of his paintings. Vincent went to a stack of canvases and pulled one that was black and grey chalk and watercolor. It was a study of an elderly lady seated in the corner sewing. Arthur studied it appreciatively looking from the painting to the same lady in the corner now knitting. He nodded and agreed to purchase it at the artist's price.

Vincent shook hands and relaxed in his seat. Sien was setting the table for lunch and to Arthur's surprise he was invited to share soup with them. He sat at the table across from Vincent and next to the boy, Next to Vincent was Sien who poured out soup and then passed a loaf of bread from which everyone broke off a piece. As they ate the conversation was about Shakespeare who Vincent felt to be the penultimate writer. Arthur had read a lot about Vincent Van Gogh, but little had spoken about how intelligent he was and how varied were his interests. Most reports dwelt on his irritable nature and financial problems.

For most of the next few hours they talked on a variety of subjects, their conversation becoming friendlier and more relaxed. This was helped by the innumerable wines they were consuming. Taking glasses and the bottle outside they sat comfortably in the cool evening. Arthur pulled out a cigar and offered one to Van Gogh. This was politely refused. The small boy, who had never been introduced, came out to get a kiss goodnight. Once kissed he ran back inside to go to sleep.

Arthur asked about the boy. "He is not my son but Sien's. I have been close to him as a father though. He is the son of one of Sien's clients." Arthur looked startled, "Clients?" Vincent slowly turned to face Arthur with the look of a man about to storm. He growled his answer menacingly, "She is a prostitueret." Arthur's look of surprise was mixed with a small amount of aversion. It irritated Van Gogh. He dashed his glass against the wall and stormed into the house muttering about how his brother, uncle and the rest all berated him for living with a prostitute.

Arthur recovered slowly then rose and made a dash for the door. It was opened as he arrived, the painting was thrust into his hands. "Take your painting and go. No money just go." The door was slammed in Arthurs's face. He made a tentative move to knock but heard Van Gogh stomping around the inside while Sien tried her best to calm him down. Arthur waited a while longer then surreptitiously made his way to the shed. The lock was undisturbed and when he opened it he got a shock. The portal was not visible. In his semi drunken state, he didn't recall the blind he had placed to conceal the open portal. In the darkness he panicked and beat on one wall after another. He was reaching a point of complete desperation when he tripped and fell through the black shield of the portal and landed face down in the studio. He had held the painting outstretched and it entered into the 21st century unharmed.

At Martins desk he pulled out the bottle of five star and poured himself a generous portion. As he sipped the warming amber whisky, he made a list of places and people to create a paper trail for his discovery of the painting. He planned that the final discovery would be in the basement storage accumulated by the previous gallery owner. Almost all of the paintings were worthless and commercial but hidden amongst the debris would be his one piece of gold!

IN THE PAST

Martin soon got tired of gesticulating into the empty air. If Arthur was there, he would have located him and opened his end. He had nothing to do now but wait the next two and a half days out. Setting the easel and paints in readiness he sketched out a view from his window. The courtyard was centered with a colorful garden. From the center a fountain sprayed a mist over the surrounding flowers and benches. Splaying out was a series of stones forming a meandering path leading to each of the apartment doorways. He dabbed colors on the canvas working with practiced ease. He noticed a circle of amber and blue that appeared momentarily and then disappeared, appearing again in a new location. Laying pallet and brushes aside he went down the back stairs for a closer look.

From the doorway he peered out over a sea of flowers. Bobbing up and down amongst the waving blooms was the amber and blue that had attracted his attention. Walking the path he worked his progress so that he and the other would intersect. They arrived together near one of the benches, The amber and blue was revealed to be a hat which covered an attractive female whose amber hair hung loose and thick over her shoulders. She let out a gasp as she bumped into Martin's legs. Looking up she was revealed as an attractive woman of over twenty but not yet thirty. She handed up the basket which Martin took and set on the bench. Assisting her to rise she straightened slowly arching her back to relieve a kink. She sat down and patted the bench in invitation for Martin to be seated.

"You are new here." She remarked without preamble. Martin nodded dumbly. He was admiring the sparkle in her eyes and the way the sides crinkled when she smiled. She cocked her head to the side. "Do you speak?" She brushed his hand and leaned towards him as she spoke. "Yes, I was in awe of your gentle beauty. I would like to paint your portrait if you would not mind." She held her hand in front of her face. You are the second who wishes to paint me. I shall become vain if I am requested as a model so often."

Martin took her hand away from her face. "And who was the other?" He held her chin in his hand. She blushed but sat straighter, "He is a great artist, he lives in the Casa Buonarroti nearby, he is Michelangelo Buonarroti." She seemed to be proud of being a model for so famous an artist. She looked over at a sundial bordered by a flowering bush. I must wash and change, he gets very angry if I am late." She rose and headed to her apartment grabbing her basket of small flowers. She stopped and turned back halfway down the path. "If you wait for me, you can escort me to his studio, perhaps you would like to make his acquaintance?" Martin bowed acknowledging he certainly would. She smiled and bounced a curtsy then dashed off to her rooms.

He lay on the bench and closed his eyes. Grinning widely, he thought about meeting his hero. With an introduction from so fair a maiden he felt sure he would at least be greeted favorably. A soft touch on his nose, he opened his eyes to be greeted by his friend laughing at him. She pulled his arm to raise him, and admonished him for sleeping.

As they walked to the studio, she introduced herself as Catarina Esposito and she was a nurse at the hospital. Today was her first day off in a week and she was going to enjoy her next three days of freedom. Today she would be a model for Michelangelo, she looked up coquettishly at Arthur, "perhaps tomorrow I can be a model for you? It will cost you though, you must give me food and drink before I will stand for you." Arthur promised he would do as she requested. As they neared the Casa Buonarroti she pulled Arthur along in her haste. At the door she knocked. The door opened and Arthur had his first look at Michelangelo.

It has been said that meeting a hero can be both daunting and sometimes even depressing. The man before him was short, only a bit over five feet. His face was long and deeply lined. The dark hair and beard framed a face that was intellectual and stern but the laugh lines beside the eyes denoted a man with humor. Martin was slightly disappointed at his first meeting but soon regained his admiration for this great man who was a leader in many fields of the renaissance,

He was invited in and asked to sit as Michelangelo situated Catarina into position for sketching. She was seated holding a long roll of paper. Her body turned partially sideways but looking directly at him. He placed a cloth over her hair and draped it around her. He sketched her quickly except for her face which he took time over getting in every nuance. When he finished, he was introduced to Arthur. Catarina glanced sideways at Martin with a sly smile as she told Michelangelo that here too was a great artist. Arthur colored as she said this, and Michelangelo's gaze turned on him reflectively. Michelangelo dragged a piece of paper in front of Arthur and dropped a handful of charcoal, pencils, and chalk nearby. "Show me."

Martin hesitated; he hadn't expected to be put to the test so quickly. He reminisced about what he thought might impress his hero. Michelangelo, he remembered, was a devotee of anatomical renderings. To show quickly that he too was adept he sketched a detailed drawing of an arm laying on a table. The hand open and palm forward, the skin of the arm stripped and laying in front. Then the muscles and tendons were done detailed and complete. He added red chalk to give depth and color and shaded with the charcoal. It was done quickly but as detailed as a photograph. He turned it to face Michelangelo and Catarina.

Catarina's face was a study of surprise and awe. She hadn't taken Martin's claims of being an artist seriously but now she looked at him with respect. Michelangelo pulled another paper in front of Arthur and requested he do a back half covered in skin the other half showing muscles. Martin smiled; this was one of his party tricks. He had done a series of anatomical renderings of various sections of the body half stripped and half intact. He could do this with his eyes shut. He didn't want to get cocky though so did the rendering as carefully as possible. He showed the grain of the muscles and the layers and connectors. It was as detailed as a diagram used for medical students. In an hour he had a full drawing done to his satisfaction.

The entire time Martin was drawing Michelangelo was working on his own drawings for the Sistine Chapel ceiling. Catarina was seated at the end of the table watching both artists working. Her arms folded on the table and her chin resting on her hands. She looked from one artist to the other with a grin of admiration on her face. Taking a scrap piece of paper, she began a sketch of her own. She enjoyed art and artists but had never tried drawing herself. Looking from one man to another she decided to sketch Martin. Her sketch lacked depth but was an accurate rendering. She broke off some chalk and did some shading. They all completed at the same time, and each looked over the others.

Martin asked if he could keep Catarina's sketch and place it on the wall of his room. Michelangelo requested to keep Arthur's drawing and invited him to return tomorrow. Arthur and Catarina admired Michelangelo's sketch and requested an opportunity to see the panel once completed. Arthur was invited to accompany Michelangelo the following morning and assist in some of the fresco work.

Leaving the studio Martin asked Catarina to join him for dinner, he allowed her to pick the restaurant. She chose a pub where you brought in the food and they would cook it and provide the wine. On the way there they bought first a basket and then dinner. A duck was selected followed by garlic, onions oranges and lettuce. Cheese was hard to find but some was eventually located as well as pears and apples.

At the pub they handed over the ingredients and sat with a carafe of wine. In the wine were spices, juices and rings of citrus fruits. Water was brought on the side to be added as wanted. Arthur sampled the wine and poured out for both of them. He asked to be told about nursing in the hospital. Apparently, she enjoyed talking about her work because she clapped her hands, leaned on the table and opened her mind.

"It's a wonderful place to work, so many doctors and so many people they can help!" Her eyes sparkled as she talked. "I go through the hospital and ensure all are as comfortable as they can be, I make sure they take their medicine and sometimes I have to scold them when they don't. There are seven of us who nurse the sick. Sometimes we get sick ourselves, but we still work, we can't lie in bed and get well so we work and get well." She shook her head, "sometimes there are people who we can't help. The nuns pray for them, but it doesn't usually help. I don't understand why."

They were interrupted in their discussion as a plate of bread, butter and cheese was brought out. The duck would continue to roast for a while longer. "What were you rooting around for in the garden?" She pulled a small flower from her pocket. "It's a type of marigold, the top you can eat and with the leaves you make into a salve for scratches." She showed her arm which had scratches running half the length." "One of our patients did this and if I use the salve it will heal faster. It also makes a soothing tea." The duck arrived and as they ate Arthur listened as she waxed lyrically over various plants she used and what they did. Dinner over they walked back to the apartments.

In his room he sketched Catarina again. His mind was becoming saturated with her. The way she looked, her enthusiasm in everything she did, her flamboyance even. He grinned to himself as he remembered the way she moved and flounced around. She was a complete extrovert and he enjoyed being with her. He lay back in his bed and dreamed of the sculptures he could make with her as a model. She was his muse and would guide him to the most glorious sculptures he could do.

IN THE PRESENT

Arthur was back at Martin's studio. He was working out his plan to "find" the missing painting. Looking through a registry of pawn shops from around the time of Van Gogh he made his list and then set up a program so he could walk through drop off the painting then turn around and pick it up around six months later.

At the first he walked in confidently and placed the picture on the counter. The man behind the counter looked the picture over, shrugged and handed it back. Martin returned it to the man with a request to pawn it. The pawnbroker put on his glasses and studied the picture again. "And how much do you wish for, this?" To Arthur's astonishment he didn't even sound interested. "Six hundred francs." The man laughed and dropped the picture on the counter pointing to the door he told Martin to get out. Arthur took the picture and held it in front of himself. "This is a Van Gogh!" he said haughtily. The pawnbroker shook at the knees and looked weak. He reached trembling hands out to retake the picture. Once holding it again, his face changed to one of derision, "And what is a Van Gogh?" Arthur colored, "He is the most famous painter in the world!" he stated, pounding a fist on the wooden counter. The man flung the picture back at Arthur.

Arthur suddenly realized his error, A great and world-famous painter was what Van Gogh would become, he wasn't one in this here and now. He apologized and asked for 10 francs. The pawnbroker looked ready to spit at Martin but shrugged and filled out a pawn slip. Martin watched as the broker laid the money on the counter, took the picture into a back room and casually flung it onto a top shelf. Upon picking it back up he found it was slightly dusty. He dashed back to the studio to dust it and take it to the next facility.

At the next it was a similar experience except the broker had heard of Van Gogh and offered a slightly higher amount. At the third things began with a difficulty,

"This seems to be, as you say a Van Gogh, but it is one I have not heard of before." He flipped through a catalogue listing art and literature. He made little grunts of disappointment as he leafed through the pages not finding the work in question. "This could be an original or it is possibly a forgery. Without more information I cannot take it in pawn." He handed it back and bowed Arthur out of the shop. Arthur slipped it back into the canvas sheath he used for covering it.

Down the street he located a gallery. Entering he made a request to store a painting in their vaults. The manager took the painting and brought it to a desk with a brighter light. Placing a Jewelers Lupe into his eye he carefully studied the painting. He looked at the brush strokes in the watercolor, he looked at the glide of chalk and the blending of charcoal. Finally, after examining it he sat back in his chair, crossed his arms over his chest and sunk his head in thought. "Where did you say you acquired this?" he asked suddenly. Arthur smiled, "I didn't say." The gallery owner looked glum as he faced Arthur. "Sir, in order to store your piece here we would need to insure it against loss. I would like to call in an expert to confirm my suspicion that this is an authentic work by Vincent Van Gogh, do I have your permission or would you like to withdraw your request. Arthur considered carefully. Having his piece confirmed and notarized in an insurance policy would greatly increase its authenticity and pedigree. He agreed with the proviso that they store it securely.

The insurance authenticator took one look at the painting and promptly fainted. A drop of brandy and cool cloths revived him. He held the picture reverently. "There can be no doubt as to its authenticity, this is a Van Gogh, possibly one of his earliest works." They set out a sum agreed upon by all as the insurance sum and Arthur received paperwork stating it as a work of Vincent Van Gogh.

Word quickly got out that a new Van Gogh had been found. While the location was not revealed it didn't take more than a day for it to be discovered. Something so incredible was bound to be spoken of and the gallery was besieged with requests to show the painting. Reporters, Newsreel men and Gossip columnists were all badgering the gallery to the point normal work was not being able to be done. In taking in the painting, he ended up losing money daily. He finally agreed to a short viewing. Police were obtained and stood on either side of the painting two behind and two in front. The picture was placed on an easel covered in a maroon silk cloth. A guard rail was placed around beyond which no one was to pass. The picture was unveiled. to a packed house.

In the present, Arthur was at the library going through microfiches. He chanced on a newspaper which told of the discovery of a previously unknown Van Gogh painting. A picture of the painting was included and full description by the gallery as to why they felt it was authentic. Arthur rushed back to the studio and set the time machine for a year later than the day he had dropped off the picture. The gallery was larger and more prestigious now. In the center of the main wall under a secure cage was his picture. Irate, he approached the counter and slammed down his paperwork. He wanted to pick up his picture.

"Sorry sir, the manager isn't in today. He has the key and we can't open it without that." Arthur leaned forward over the counter. "Call him." Two short words but the threat behind them was understood. The man called the manager. The manager arrived quickly but didn't seem anxious to release the painting. "Sir, we can secure your painting very well as you can see. We have followed your instructions and it is completely safe." Arthur was not swayed, "I can see that, but I have need of my picture now. Please remove it from its casing so that I can get it home." The manager reached into his pocket fingering the keys. "Sir, you never did say how you acquired this painting. Such a work should.." Arthur stepped closer to the man and growled. "The Picture."

One of the clerks, seeing the threatening visage and stance put in a discrete call to the police. When they arrived Arthur and the manager were still arguing. "What's all this then?" he inquired. It took several minutes to sort things out as both men were speaking over each other. Arthur pulled out his paperwork and the manager was stating that there was no proof of ownership and that the picture could have been stolen. "Arthur stated that it had been in his family since it was given to his cousin in 1881. The officer hemmed and hawed a bit then suggested that since the gallery had insured and accepted the picture on Arthur's word alone it would have to be returned to him. Very reluctantly the gallery manager climbed a short ladder, unlocked the cage and brought the picture out.

Arthur briskly retrieved his property and thanking the officer, made his way to where he had left the portal opened.

In the studio he boxed up the picture and carted it back to his office. He took several photos, printed them out and added copies of all the documentation. Putting everything between two pieces of cardboard he slid the package into an envelope. Whistling as he trotted down the stairs he sauntered down the street to the post box. With a heart beating hard he opened the door to slide in the envelope when he was forcefully prevented. A heavy hand thudded on his shoulder, he was swept backwards. The envelope went flying and Arthur was slammed against the cold brick of an apartment building. The envelope was adroitly caught in midair by his assailant.

When the grey mist faded from Arthurs eyes, he was helped up from his slumped position by the same person who had just assaulted him. Holding him carefully they walked together to the rear entrance of the gallery and up the back steps to his office. Seated behind his desk he watched as the other man got them both a whiskey then unwrapped himself from his scarf and took off his coat.

It's an odd thing to see oneself in person without the aid of a mirror. He sat down opposite Arthur and dropped the envelope on the desk. Arthur looked with undisguised interest at this man before him. It was himself, there was no doubt but the face was scarred, there was a bandage on the right temple and the shirt was torn and stained. He looked tired and worst of all, angry. "YOU DAMN FOOL!" He shouted. "You can't do anything right can you. You almost cost me everything including my freedom, do you realize that you jackass!" His other self-rose and pulled the picture and paperwork out placing them between them he spread them apart, He began to enumerate the situation:

1. You signed with your own name on all of these, 1882 to 2022 congratulations you're the oldest man alive!

2. You didn't age any of these, they're all fresh and new.

3. You never thought to check if the picture you got back was the one you gave them, did you. It's a copy you ass!

Tired of being abused both physically and verbally he leapt over the desk and dove into his future self. Both men were obviously equally matched, but his future self had an edge. He was angry and adrenaline was surging. As they struggled his future self was landing strike after strike while exclaiming, "Stop hitting yourself, stop hitting yourself." Realizing they were both behaving like idiots, they separated. Arthur of the present sat on the edge of his desk. A moment later what his future self said hit home about it being a copy.

Arthur gawped and went over to behind the couch where he had hastily placed the picture. It was a good copy he had to admit. The brush work was tentative and not with the smooth strokes of the original, the charcoal was of a different mixture and the pencil was lighter. He put his head in his hands while his other self paced the floor. "I was almost charged with fraud once Sotheby realized it wasn't an original. The police raided the gallery and I just escaped out of the attic and made a dash for the studio. Now that I've prevented you from making a major boner lets sort things out so I can go back.

FRESCO

Martin woke early the next day. He lay in bed relaxed and comfortable. As the morning light filtered in and crossed his bed he decided to rise and if possible, shine. Emptying the water pitcher into a bowl he bathed as best he could and put on the clothes he had worn yesterday. He checked his collection of jewels and decided to take two along in case he wanted to buy some more clothes. He tucked what money he had left into a leather pouch and tied it onto his belt.

Looking out the window he saw Catarina in a corner of the garden that was piled with kitchen scraps left to decompose. She was putting something into a pot and seemed to be inspecting them carefully only picking the best of something or other. Curious and wanting to see if she would accompany him for breakfast before going to see Michelangelo, he dashed down the stairs and ran over to where she was crouched.

"Good morrow fair maiden," he exclaimed as he approached. Rather that was what he had wanted to exclaim but the pungent aroma of decay caused the words to choke in his throat. She looked around at the sound of his gasping retches and giggled beneath her mask. She had taken a kerchief and soaked it in vinegar to combat the stench. She rose and showed him her pot full of grubs. She led him to a bench. "These are for wounds and will speed healing very nicely. I have to bring some into the hospital. A day off means nothing when you work for the church." She looked sideways as she spun the grubs in the pot. "Are you going to see Michelangelo this morning?" Martin acknowledged that he was indeed planning on seeing him. The chance to be part of the team painting the Sistine Chapel was too good an opportunity to miss.

She pouted looking at him with mock disappointment, "and here I had hoped to model for you." She raised her skirt to show a shapely leg "No? then perhaps tomorrow unless of course you do not wish to see me as eve was on the first day." She laughed at his embarrassment then her mood changed to serious. "Tell me, do you like me?" Martin took her hand, "Very much so. You are more different than any woman I have ever known." He was troubled in his mind though, "Tell me, are you being truthful to me or am I just someone to flirt with." She suddenly turned and sat facing him. She stroked his cheeks and holding his head she leant over and kissed him. The kiss was warm, gentle, loving. When they parted, she tilted her head. "Now do you think I am just flirting with you. I want to be your muse. I want to inspire you to your best work!"

Martin realized that she had been inspiring him since their first meeting. He had done sketch after sketch of her in his mind and on paper. Her image was in front of him continually. He drew her close and kissed her again. "You are my muse and through you I will be all that I have ever wanted to be." She stood with the pot of maggots in one hand holding his hand with the other. "Promise me tomorrow we will be together." Martin stood and held her close, "Tomorrow is for us." She slid out of his arms and danced to the door of her apartment, At the door she turned, curtsied, and blew him a kiss.

Martin was walking in a daze of confused emotions to meet with Michelangelo. To his surprise he was greeted by him and a bevy of his apprentices as they made their way to the Sistine Chapel. He fell in behind the group and got in step. One of the apprentices reached into a bag and handed Martin a roll of cloth, inside were various tools for the days undertaking. Martin whistled happily as they made their way along quiet streets. As they made their way down the street Martin was admiring an ornate chapel they were about to pass. On the steps stood an older man and entourage. As Michelangelo passed, he called out to the man, "Hey Leonardo, when will you finish the horse?" His apprentices joined in the laughter.

Leonardo Da Vinci stomped in rage as his followers' cast epithets at Michelangelo and company. One of Leo's followers ran up and pulled Martin by the sleeve, swinging him around. Martin's tools fell as he spun. In his anger he lashed out, a right hook to the young man's jaw sent him sprawling. Another man rushed to his compatriot's aid only to be felled by a blow to the chest that sent him stumbling backwards. This was too much for Leonardo who sent his company into the fray. Arriving grouped together they overwhelmed Martin from all sides. He went down under a barrage of blows. As suddenly as it had started. The men scurried away leaving Martin in a heap in the road bleeding and bruised.

He was found by a passing Carabinieri who picked him up and carried him to the Hospital. Waking from his stupor he struggled to get his bearings. His memory was clear to the point when he had succumbed to the furious attack. Now he was in a bed and bandaged. Beside him was a clay pitcher and cup of water. Turning to the right, he saw Catarina on a chair sleeping with her head on the mattress softly snoring. With difficulty he reached over and stroked her head. A nun passing by in the customary habit in black and white and seeing Martin awake offered to bring him some soup. She looked at Catarina affectionately, "She has been by your side for two days, ever since you came in. She should wake soon so I will bring soup for both of you. She left with so graceful a walk that she seemed to be floating.

Catarina woke to Martins gentle touch. She took his hand and kissed it. "You missed our meeting!" She scolded with mock seriousness. Martin began to apologize when she placed a finger on his lips. The soup and bread arrived quickly; they ate in silence. Martin was amazed that she had stayed with him as he slept and recovered. Catarina was surprised at the depth of her feelings. She had fallen for Martin at first sight and her feelings had become deeper every time she saw him. As he ate Martin tried to sort out his feelings for Catarina. The change from the pleasure of having her as a companion to something more meaningful had happened within moments. She was beautiful in a way he could appreciate. She had an enthusiasm for life and whatever she did he found delightful. She was so energetic it was like watching a humming bird as she darted around from stall to stall while they had been shopping. He smiled to himself as he thought of their unusual dinner the previous night.

Sudden realization struck him. Not the previous night, that was two days ago. Recollection flooded his mind. He had been unconscious for two nights making four all together. He had missed the rendezvous. Hopefully Arthur was working the plan they had established. If so, he only had to go to the drop off point and wait. He sat up and struggled to get out of bed. Catarina attempted to push him back in. For a few minutes they had a battle of wills. Martin held her and explained, "Catarina, I am late for a very important meeting that will mean a lot for both of us. I have to go and go alone, if not I am lost." She stepped back and looked at him with tears in her eyes. "Go then. you know where I will be."

She turned hurt eyes towards him before walking away, "If you still want me." He heard her mutter aloud as she walked off. He hurriedly got dressed and finding everything including his purse, he placed a small sapphire on the pillow and rushed out. The nun was surprised to find them both gone and even more surprised when she found the small blue stone centered on the pillow.

Leaving the hospital at top speed he was forced to slow down. He had not allowed himself to recover completely and it showed. He reached the rendezvous spot out of breath and in a great deal of pain. He hoped he wouldn't have to wait too long for Arthur to open the portal. His wait was short after all and as the portal opened, he dove through and landed in his studio tears falling on the floor that were not all from pain.

Arthur helped him to stand. "Pal, what the hell have you done to yourself!" He sat Martin down and poured him a shot. Martin declined the liquor in favor of water and a few aspirin. Arthur perched on the side of the desk and smiled at his friend. "It's damn good to have you back pal, but like I asked, what the hell have you done to yourself?" Martin leaned back and stretched his legs hoping the aspirins would kick in soon. "Well, I met Michelangelo soon after moving into my place. Met a young lady who I enjoy being with a lot, had a fight with Leonardo Da Vinci's gang and spent a few days in hospital sleeping. Other than that, not much. What have you been up to? He looked up and realized that Arthur looked a lot different than he had four days ago.

"Well, you've actually been gone for a year. Kind of anyway. Soon after you left, I found out the storm had caused a hell of a leak in the gallery attic. I was fortunate to be able to use the machine to get the stuff secured before it had been ruined, which it had been. Then when I was cleaning out the storage in the basement, I found an old painting which I hadn't seen before. It took me a while to research it and send it off to be authenticated. I sold it for a few bucks." He handed over an envelope with a thousand in hundred-dollar bills. "That's your cut." Martin was surprised, He'd never gotten a cut from one of Arthur's sales before unless it was something of his.

He was about to comment but Arthur shushed him and placed the money in his pocket. Martin decided not to pursue the matter but was curious about it being a year later. "Martin, I spent a hell of a long time trying to find you. For most of the year I searched streets and alleys, courtyards, and every building within a ten-mile radius. It was incredibly frustrating. I knew you couldn't have walked very far but I just couldn't find you. I kicked myself when I realized I had worked this the wrong way. All I had to do was stay on the meet up place and just shunt the portal open at regular intervals. Sure enough, when I went back to a couple of days after the initial meeting, and you weren't there I just kept opening and closing the portal until you barreled through." He had lied and lied so well that Martin was convinced and seemed willing to drop the subject.

Relieved that things had gone so smoothly he didn't feel the need to mention that he had made over five million on the Van Gogh painting. What he had given Martin was nominal. He smiled inwardly as he thought of the other artists he planned to meet early in their career. He would become the master at finding early works of the greatest artist in the world. Smoothing his expensive suit, he shook hands with Martin offering to take him out to dinner later that evening allowing him to get reacquainted with everything again.

Martin walked along the shelves noticing dust covering everything. Disappointed that Arthur hadn't kept the studio up he did a quick dust and sweep. Bringing a box of various components from the original portal, he set about creating a miniature one. Building one in a six-by-six frame was no problem. He was able to use a laser pointer to create the portal. Now all he needed was a small unit to keep it homed in on his lodgings in Italy of the past. He duplicated the first as a companion to be used in Italy. If correct it should create a window where he would receive internet from the future. He fervently hoped it worked as he didn't want to come back again and find that a year or more had passed again. He set Realtime to work on figuring out the coordinates and times to link the two units together and imbed onto a microchip in the frame. Once activated they would remain open.

Giving himself a quick wash and brush he dressed in the best he had for dinner. Arthur had promised him a real treat at a fancy restaurant in Chicago! After a dinner at Chez Paul with wine served with every course, Martin was dropped off at his studio. Martin had said he would be gone by the morning and that if everything worked out, he'd be dropping up every now and then. He'd leave a date, time, and coordinates for a pickup if anything went wrong. In order to test that they functioned as he wanted, he placed the units six feet apart and tossed a pencil through one frame. He was delighted when it came immediately out the second. He left a list of instructions for

Arthur in case his units failed, however he did not inform him where the small portal was. One unit he placed high on a shelf near the router tucked away and hidden. Plugged in, it opened the portal. He made a quick run to the bank depositing the money then bought some more jewels including a nice emerald ring for Catarina.

He opened Realtime again at the location they had used before. Stepping through with a satchel containing everything he would need for a while he stepped through with crossed fingers. Turning he watched the portal close and fade out. Now was the time to see if he could get back. Rushing to his apartment he bolted the door and stuffed a sandal under the door to act as a further block. He brought out the unit and plugged it into his power supply. The mini portal opened. Peering through he could see into the studio. Rubbing his hands in glee he opened the easel and pulled out all the slots to create his own portal. He plugged in the laptop and turned it on.

He relaxed in his chair as the laptop ran through the boot sequence. He loaded Realtime and waited, and waited some more. Puzzled he looked over to see there was no internet again. He cursed as he saw the mini portal had shut down. Together they were drawing too much power. He bolted outside. Wandering the shops he found another pot, copper rods, cork and some vinegar. Once separated it powered the mini portal but would deplete rapidly. He powered up his portal. Bringing over an hourglass he timed how long he could leave everything open. The mini portal lasted twenty minutes. The easel portal for half an hour. He set the batteries to recharge. Marking off on a sheet he worked out how many times he could recharge his "batteries" before needing to change out the vinegar. Each depletion shortened the time open by seven minutes. Recharge took two hours no matter what.

He would have to find an alternative battery fluid that would last longer and charge faster. Until then, he would use the portal sparingly and only when absolutely necessary. He put the satchel on a shelf. Inside was a bottle of whisky, a rolled up newspaper, 15 bars of chocolates, 5 twinkies and 4 jars of instant coffee. He changed and went out to buy some new clothes before he saw Catarina again. When he eventually knocked on her door, he was dressed in the finest clothes he had. He had a large bouquet of flowers, a basket of fruit, and the ring. The door opened and she jumped into his arms sending fruit flying and crushing the flowers.

MONET

Arthur drove back to the Gallery in his Bentley Continental. Smoking a cigar he contemplated his next coup. After his previous error that cost his future self dearly, he had become more careful. Together they had worked out a means to acquire paintings at definitive times in an artist's career. By getting one at a cusp point it would usually be able to be purchased cheaply. By getting it within two hundred years of the present he could work the trail easier. He had already worked out with his future self a series of hiding places to age receipts and various personas for each time he would be storing or pawning the artworks. With a plan in place, he could make millions more.

The gallery had expanded taking over the storefront next door. Here were the local artists leaving the main gallery for works that were being sent in from all over. He had the opportunity to be choosy and chose only the cream. Passing through the gallery he was saluted by those that worked there and he nodded to the many patrons in search of fine art. Upstairs in his office he sat behind his ornate desk and started his new listing of times, places and artists to visit. Eventually he hoped to be able to accomplish the sales himself eliminating the commission that Sotheby charged. He was becoming avarice. The name Claude Monet was thrumming in his mind. He recalled that Monet had entered his work in many exhibitions where few sold. With a thousand francs he could pick one or two up. He practiced the various signatures he would use as he had a new scheme of the painting going from one collector to another finally landing the painting in his hands. The letters would lie in the numerous locations which would age them. Once gathered he would send off the painting with copies of the letters for official authentication. In time his word alone would be all that was needed.

From the corner of his desk, he poured himself a drink out of a cut glass decanter. The rich amber fluid warmed him as he unwrapped another cigar and walked to the large plate glass window. He looked out over the street below. The tree lined streets, old fashioned apartment buildings and ancient streetlights made for a pleasant view from here. He could look across the street and up to the window of his new apartment. This was more like the life he had envisioned for himself. Still, he thought, the best was yet to be!

Scouring the internet on clothes of the period he wrote a description of what he would need. Visiting thrift stores put him in hand of several suits that could be adjusted to meet the period. Taking his package of items to the studio he brought out scissors, hemming tape, an iron and ironing board. With a little effort he had a suit of clothes that were similar enough to pass muster. Setting the portal to open near a secluded area near the Rue des Capucines, he scouted around for the salon where Monet and others held their exhibitions.

Passing an entrance with a line extended outside and down the street he walked to the end and stood with the rest. As the line progressed, he approached a jeweler. Breaking his place in line he sold a diamond for another two thousand francs. In fifteen minutes, he entered the salon.

No amount of conjecture prepared him for what was inside. Chandeliers flooded the interior with illumination. Three-legged stands covered the floor mounted paintings. On small tables stood selections of sculptures. Each artist sat in the center of their works. Some artists had both paintings and sculptures. From a corner he counted thirty artists and over a hundred and fifty works. Flushed with excitement he looked around taking in the works of such luminaries as Monet, Degas, Renoir. He paid his entrance fee of one franc and wandered around like a kid in a candy store.

From Degas he purchased several of the minor works of the From a Cotton Office in New Orleans series for a hundred and fifty francs each. Renoirs were purchased for three hundred francs. He was tempted by Monet's Impression of Sunrise opting rather quickly for a lesser version. While paler in colors it still was worth having. This was had for one hundred rather than the thousand he wanted for the better version. He found a few others and a sculpture from a Delantour which he was practically given at twenty five francs.

As he looked for more works to purchase, he passed what he took for a newsman writing his views. A glance at the notes showed utter disdain for the works. He called them unfinished, confusing and without value. With so many people wandering the salon he was astonished how few sales were made. Apparently, many others shared the newsman's opinions.

Tying his paintings together and placing the sculpture under his arm he scurried away with his treasures. He made several more sorties until he had spent all three thousand. He opened the portal into the basement of the Gallery and placed his works into a new locker added for the purpose. Only he had the key, and it would stay that way. He set the timer to close the computer and walked from the basement up to his office. Under his arm was one of the Renoirs. He put it onto a Locking mini easel on his desk that had an intense light and magnifier attached. Examining it closely he began his write up and started to create the paper trail he needed. He was determined to do this himself by writing papers of transmission from one owner to another. Some were to be letters, some receipts, some as notices. Each was to be accomplished in a different hand. These would be placed in locations to age and then picked up in the present.

A knock on the door and Marta entered before he could answer. As the floor manager she usually consulted him about items to change out on the floor. She entered with a notebook and pen. He dodged around trying to block her view of the painting. Focusing only on her list and taskings she sat down on the opposite side of the desk while Arthur tried to regain his composure and answer her inquiry. She laid her pad on the desk in front of him. "We have quite a few items that are not getting any interest. I have listed items to replace them with." Arthur looked over the list and added a few items he would like placed on the floor. "Since we're going more upscale and including more of the classics, let's include a few of Martin's sculptures that have been locked away for months. In the new scheme they might sell now." Marta smiled. Arthur's allegiance to Martin's works was one of the things that showed a soft spot in an otherwise stern demeanor.

As she gathered her pad her elbow nudged the Renoir sending it tilting back so it faced her. Her gasp brought Arthur out of his reverie, and he quickly turned it back around. "Sorry Marta but I'm getting frustrated with this one. I can't tell if it's authentic or a very good fake. It's starting to get to me." Since she had seen it, he turned it round to face her. "What would you say?" She looked at it carefully. Going to a shelf she pulled out a book of Renoir's paintings. "It's either a copy or an early attempt at this one." She turned the book towards Arthur. He looked it over, "I agree that it might be an early attempt. I'm pretty darn sure it's authentic though." She rose and smiled, "If it is, you will do well not to sell it but give it a home here. It will bring more people in, they will buy the others. Find more as this and you will be the Indiana Jones of the art world!" Arthur rose and escorted her out admonishing her not to tell anyone about it until he had its authenticity confirmed.

Working on the few letters took most of the day continuing into the evening. He triple checked them then waited. When his future self didn't show up, he made his way to the studio. Working with a list he placed the letters in various drops through time then turned around and picked them up in the present. "Aged to perfection!" he acknowledged joyfully. Packing them up he headed out. Stopping for a moment he looked around the studio. He chanced on the picture Martin had sketched out from his trip to Italy. It was of a lady painting in detail, the people were blurred. There in the background was a clock and archway.

With a sense of DeJa'Vu he peered closer. There was something very familiar about it, he just couldn't figure out why. Wracking his mind he sought an image that was elusive, always seeming just out of reach. He shrugged, went outside and locked the studio. Jiggling the door, he made sure it was secure. Tomorrow he would post the letters and a picture of the painting. Lounging in his comfortable desk chair he considered his position. "Maybe Marta was right, maybe I ought to keep this one and put it in a prominent place in the studio. I have others to auction. This might be just what is needed to improve the galleries reputation." Using some of these artworks as a catalyst to bring people in might just be what was wanted.

PAST TO THE PRESENT

Martin was surprised at the warm welcome. Surmising correctly, he felt she must have thought he was making excuses to drop her. She dragged him inside her apartment and made him lunch. She filled him with salad, rustic bread, chicken and wine. Looking around he was surprised at how Spartan it was. While similar to his own place there was ornamentation based solely on her faith, medical knowledge, and simplicity. Over the bed was a cross. By the bed was a small prayer stool covered in a tapestry of the hospital. A large ornate mirror hung by the door. Shelves of medicinal plants filled the room with fragrance and color. In the corner was a small stove and the table and chairs where he was seated.

When they had eaten, he helped to clear the table and wash the crockery. It amused her that he was willing and ready to help her. "May we go to your apartment now? it is time for me to inspire you." Her eyes twinkled with mischief as she led him outside. He led the way to his apartment and bowed as he ushered her inside. On various scraps of paper were his sketches of her as she had been seen from the window. "You see? I am already inspiring you." She pulled a chair close to the easel and waited for him to position her.

He sat her slightly sideways. A smile broke on his lips, He dashed out the door to go to the garden and her apartment. She could hear the thump of his steps as he jumped every other one. She maintained her position patiently though she was curious as to what he was doing. He arrived with a handful of small flowers and a handkerchief filled with grubs as well as a few potted plants from her home. From a pocket he brought dandelions which he plaited into her hair. The flowers were held in her hands and the grubs were kept in the handkerchief on her lap. On the floor he gathered the medicinal plants. She had to continually nudge the grubs into place and retrieve the ones that had fallen. That is until Martin found a small bowl and placed a few inside. The rest he returned to their mound. Satisfied that what interested her was represented he sketched. He took the mirror from the wall to bounce light and give an almost halo like burnish to her hair as the light reflected over her.

She was a good model. She didn't fidget and held her expression. Martin worked quickly so she could relax but still kept details for whatever he decided to do with them. When she spoke she did so without moving her lips. Martin was tempted to make her a ventriloquist doll. She'd be a natural. A knock at the door startled her and sent grubs flying. Puzzled he went to see who could be calling. As he opened the door Catarina was bent picking up the grubs and returning them to the bowl. She looked up to see a gentleman dressed as a doctor, standing looking at her with amusement. "Pappi!" She exclaimed and the grubs went flying again. It just wasn't a good day to be a grub. She practically dragged her father inside and introduced him to Martin. "Martino, this is my father Pietro Delagatori."

He bowed and shook hands, "I apologize for disturbing your work. I see my daughter so seldom even though we both work at the hospital. I went to her apartment and found the note saying she had come here." Glancing around the apartment he walked to the easel and admired the sketches.

"Catarina said she had met a great artist. I thought it was one I might know." Martin stacked the sketches and intimated for her father to sit. "I have just recently arrived in Italy and am as yet unknown here." Her father held one of the sketches to the window. "Would you be able to do a large sculpture of this?" He held out the picture. While similar to the others, this had more of her smile than the rest. The eyes were wide, her joy showed through. "Certainly, how large did you have in mind." He spaced out about three feet square with his hands. "How much would you charge? I would like to place it in the hospital. The patients would like to see this." Martin considered, "Since it will be in the Hospital if you buy the marble, I will carve it for free." The two men shook hands and Catarina clapped. She felt as though she was about to become famous!

The next morning Pietro, Catarina and Martin went searching for the right stone for the sculpture. As they walked Catarina was showing signs of someone with a secret she was bursting to let out. She walked around impatiently as selecting the marble was a time-consuming business. Martin was looking at color, softness, grain. All things that would make or mar a sculpture. Once picked he was at a loss where to have it sent to. He could work outside by erecting a canopy over it. Now, Catarina's secret exploded. She moved the men aside and had them send it to Michelangelo's studio. "He has agreed to let you use his studio for sculpting! He was impressed with your sketches and is curious to see you sculpt. He is busy with the chapel so you will have access to all his tools!" She was so happy she turned a pirouette and hugged her father and Martin. Thanking Pietro, he rushed off to thank Michelangelo.

At the studio Martin was profuse in his thanks. "Master Michelangelo, Catarina has told me of your generosity. I do not know how to repay such kindness." He shook Michelangelo's hand until he had nearly shaken it off. Michelangelo patted him on the shoulder, "You wish to work with me, you respect me as a teacher and friend. For these reasons I offer this to you. My studio is yours, let it inspire you to greatness." Michelangelo gathered his requirements for the day's work. Returning, he suddenly gripped him tightly bringing him close. "You are here as my friend and student, do not compete with your master. Do not be a Leonardo who is my enemy. You are my friend because you defended me against that catso." With a final seriously threatening look Michelangelo left.

Martin brought a chair outside and waited. It wasn't long before the marble arrived in great state. Four workers arrived with it on a cart, Catarina and Pietro leading the way. Michelangelo had given Martin a corner by a window. On a table next to the stand was a complete set of hammers and chisels, a leather apron and a stack of rags. A broom was nearby intimating that he was to keep his area clean. Martin was curious as to how they would get the marble onto the base. The carts back came down and round dowels were laid in grooves. A lever raised the marble and more dowels were used to push it onto the back. It slid down onto the dowels taken from the cart to the base and positioned as Martin requested. Though working with primitive equipment they worked efficiently and expertly. Martin tipped them to their surprise and they left thanking him profusely.

Seated with some wires and wax he began to create his model. Pietro left to go to the hospital with Catarina. At the door Catarina turned and ran back to kiss Martin goodbye. She joined her father, As they walked out he heard Pietro say "I like him" to Catarina who simply let out a long sigh. Working without a break he had the model built in a few hours. A thought suddenly struck him on a way to add a signature to his work in this time without actually signing it. He had always sculpted, drawn or painted a house martin into all his works. At the time he thought of it he had considered it a stroke of genius. If Arthur ever saw one from this time, he would see it and understand. Hadn't Arthur always said his sculptures would be worth a lot if they were from years ago.

He debated a while on where to place the bird. His first thought was on her shoulder, then on the lap looking at the grubs, finally he placed it on the hem of her skirt looking up and singing. The model completed he began to rough out the marble for the following days' work. By evening he was tired. He stopped off at café to have something to eat. Tonight he dined on fish, asparagus, bread and cheese. He ate ravenously when it arrived. He hadn't had anything all day. When inspiration was strong, he worked until tired and rarely thought about food.

Walking back to the apartment he picked up some bread, cheese and wine along with some fruit to bring to Catarina. Knocking on her door he was surprised she wasn't in, or if she was, she was a sound sleeper. He left the basket on a bench outside her door and went to check if she was still working at the hospital. If she wasn't too tired, maybe they could take an evening walk. He asked after her but the response was negative. She had left hours ago. Disappointed, he walked wearily home. She had either gone to bed early and was now sound asleep or maybe she was out with her father. He knocked again on her door. Receiving no answer, he took the basket up to his room. He'd just have to give it to her tomorrow.

He opened the door to his room and received a surprise when a cold meal was waiting for him under a cloth on the table. A bigger surprise met his eyes when he noticed Catarina asleep in his bed.

The next morning Arthur woke with his arms around Catarina. She was already awake and was resting with her arms on his chest and a mile wide grin on her lips. They breakfasted on the uneaten meal she had laid out the night before. While he washed and prepared for work, she rushed downstairs to her apartment to wash and fill a basket with choice morsels to take along. She hadn't asked but she was determined to accompany him.

She might not be able to help but she could be with him and perhaps do some sketching. She felt she might even try her hand at painting and maybe learn to sculpt. With a full basket she staggered out of the apartment and met Martin coming out of his. He took the basket. Realizing by the heft she was determined to come along, he held out his arm and grasped her hand. All the way she hummed a dance tune and jigged her way up the walk.

"What do you think of your sculpture?" She turned the wax model over in her hand and then looked carefully at the face. It was just as she had seen it on the sketch. Overflowing with emotion she kissed Martin, making it last. She handed it back with eyes gleaming. "Get to work!" For the rest of the day he knocked chunks and splinters out of the marble. She was fascinated at how fast he could work on a roughing. By evening he had begun to put details on her head and face. Pietro showed up on his way home and seeing a light inside opened the door a little and peered inside. Seeing Martin was working on an intricate portion he quietly closed the door.

For the next three days Martin worked from morning until night. The sculpture was almost completed when Michelangelo approached with an offer. Marco was talented at painting marble. He needed more practice though. Would Martin allow him to paint "la infermiera"? When he hesitated Michelangelo reassured him that it would not spoil the sculpture but enhance it. Though still reluctant he felt it would not do to insult his mentor by casting doubts on one he had recommended. That evening Marco had Catarina stand in a good light so he could capture her. He made paint marks on wood listing where the colors would go. Her dress, shawl and the rest he could do from his imagination.

In the morning Martin and Catarina were too nervous to eat but rushed to the studio to see the sculpture. Opening the door, they saw Marco asleep in front of the statue, a drop cloth covered him and a mound of clay acted as a pillow. Looking down with a smile of sweetness sat the statue, looking so realistic they were in awe. Martin was in tears as he beheld one of his works he considered to be worthy of a place in history. Few people would ever see this but those who did would be inspired. Catarina rushed to the Hospital to fetch her father. Martin hated to wake Marco, but he was overcome with emotion. "You like it?" Marco inquired nervously. Martin put on a stern and disappointed appearance. "No." he replied. Marco looked ready to cry so Martin put a stop to his game and expressed his complete and utter admiration for Marco's work.

He handed over a small but excellent emerald. Marco professed his gratitude a hundred ways and sped out to change it into money.

When Pietro arrived with bearers to move the statue he stared in admiration. He sternly admonished the carters to take the utmost care of the statue and to convey it as slowly as needed to see no harm came to it. Martin was curious how they would move the statue onto and off the cart. They took hammered a wooden wedge under the base at two points then pushed a dowel through. The back was then raised and the statue rolled forward as dowels were placed in front for it to move on. Within moments the statue was loaded and all four men began the arduous task of moving it to the hospital. Catarina and Martin followed in their wake grinning like a Cheshire cat. At the Hospital, La Infermiera was placed on its base near the fountain. Within seconds it was surrounded by admirers. Martin gathered Catarina to him and was about to kiss her when he realized he was in part of a monastery. "Come," he said holding out his hand, "we have much to celebrate."

FUTURE TO THE PAST

Marta ran up the stairs to Arthur's office, burst through the door, grabbed his arm and dragged him downstairs. At the back door a large crate was being unloaded and brought into an open space. Marta turned on the lights and aimed a couple of spots. From a shelf she brought over a crowbar and handed it to Arthur. He was looking in the envelope at a letter from Italy. A large sculpture had been discovered and it was requested that Arthur, who was a leading mind on classical sculptures, to please evaluate it. Their own experts could not recognize the artist. It had a was found within a mile of Michelangelo's studio. He felt the usual irritation that every sculpture found in Italy must be from Michelangelo. Didn't they realize how many other sculptors there were back then? They said they had also found evidence that it had once been painted which was something Michelangelo never did.

Marta was unable to contain her excitement and was rapidly uncrating the sculpture. Pushing away the debris she aimed another spot so that even dirty the sculpture gleamed. "over 450 years old" Martin muttered. He brought out a magnifier from a leather case and examined the face. "I thought it might be another Madonna, but the face is different. Not the sublime expression but one of undisguised joy." He worked down to the flowers in her lap. "Small delicate blooms and why the hell are there grubs in a bowl! I don't get that." Marta seated on a stool was making notes of Arthurs observations. "Marta, you go bird watching, what bird do you make this out as?" She took the glass and scrutinized the bird. With a high-powered lens added she was able to discern faint traces of browns and blue. The tail was curved inward ending in two points. Short and squat she yelled out suddenly. "Martin!" "Martin? Marta what are you talking about?" She put the magnifiers into a drawer, "Not your friend," she laughed, "the birds a House Martin. They are in Italy as well as United States. In fact, they are pretty well everywhere."

Taking plenty of pictures he was ready to try and do whatever research he could. There wasn't much except finding that the items surrounding the figure were all part of the medicinal treatment of the time. Further down the letter it stated the figure was found where a monastery hospital used to be. He mentally tagged it as "the nurse". He checked through his books on renaissance artists. The work was such as a master would accomplish. This wasn't the work of an apprentice or student. If so then the artist had to be someone he should know. He looked again at the figure of the nurse. Everything coincided with something medical except the martin. Why the heck would they put a bird in? A photographer once told him that everything in a picture is part of the story. A sculpture should be the same. He did some research on birds and their associations with professions. Nope, nada, zip. Damn it, what did a martin have to do with it.

As if in a daze he rose and left the gallery. He drove to the studio. On the shelves were small sculptures Martin had done. Some were for sale, and some were personal. On the top shelf a small figure stood alone. Closest to his desk was one he had done early in his career, almost at the very beginning. A bird sitting in a nest, its mouth open to receive a worm or in song. He looked it over carefully and noticed similarities to the sculpture at the gallery. It was a house martin. Could it also be a signature? Artists had ways of signing their work without using their names. This might be Martins signature. There was only one way to find out.

He dug in his pocket for the letter. It had coordinates of where the hospital had been. He went there in real time. He placed the portal inside a sewer as the most secure area he could find. He felt he really ought to get with Martin about creating some better way to control the portal while traveling. There had to be a way to utilize a portal without leaving it open. He considered it very slack of Martin to not have thought of that for himself. For the moment his precautions meant either going into the sewers or somewhere high enough to avoid detection. Well, hopefully that would come soon enough. Climbing out of the sewer he went to the excavation.

From the outside you wouldn't have noticed anything wrong. The majority of the building was intact with high wooden doors in front and four spaced evenly down each side. Ornate scroll work surmounted the columns and originally the stones had been covered. Probably in some form of wattle. He opened the door peering inside then entered. It took a while for his eyes to adjust. The only light was coming through openings near the ceiling. The sun filtered by dust showed golden beams at regular intervals. He could see the archaeologists scraping away at the remains of a fountain which was next to a freestanding alcove. Arthur sneezed which brought him to the attention of the lead archeologist, an old acquaintance.

"Mr. Arthur Peterson! You must have taken the Concord!" The lead archaeologist laughed. "Had we known you wished to visit our site we would have arranged reservations for you."

Arthur acknowledged the pleasantry with a nod and bow. "Thanks Carl but I can't stay long, I just wanted to see where the statue had been." He was shown the excavation towards the front center of the vast interior where the remains of a fountain were being uncovered and labeled. To the side was an intact freestanding alcove that had protected the statue when it was buried. Portions of the second floor collapsed many years ago and taken portions of the walls out with them. The ceiling was still intact but heavily braced. Seeing nothing that interested him he made a quick survey mentally noting where things were. Then to give meaning to his visit he expressed interest in what else they had found. He was shown frescos on the walls and bits of marble reliefs that had been shattered but were slowly being pieced together. He watched as several students working on the ornate jigsaw puzzle. Each piece was photographed then numbered and placed on a sheet with others. It amused him when they became very excited to see two pieces linked and a picture forming.

"Sorry to interrupt you but I think I might have some information you might be interested in. He brought out his notebook. "We're looking at the sculpture as being sometime in the early to middle 1600's. I believe it was sculpted by Martino Conti. A little-known sculpture who worked for a time with Michelangelo then branched out on his own." Arthur was going out on a limb without a net but if his surmise was right, it might be the start of big things for himself. He could be the discoverer of another great artist. He could write books about this Martino and go on talk shows. He would become famous! "I'd like to keep the piece for study, would you mind?" The archeologist hesitated. His features went from friendly to stern as he ushered Arthur into a shed he used as an office and wrote out a letter of agreement with date of return written prominently.

"Mr. Peterson, many of our most prized possessions are scattered across the globe. We have been more fortunate than some other ancient cultures but what belongs to Italy should remain with her. I will give you three months for study, then the sculpture must be returned." Martin agreed. Taking the letter, he promised that along with the sculpture he would provide paperwork on its lineage. The two men shook hands. Now it was time to visit Martin and hear his side of the story. Arthur looked for a shop that sold Renaissance clothing reproductions. Fortunately, it wasn't difficult to find. Dressed as a well to do gentleman he put his belongings into a pouch, put his clothes in the bag and climbed down into the sewer. Thankfully, the portal was still open, and he had arrived just in time. The water in the sewer was rising. He dashed through just as it was about to pour over the edge.

Setting the portal for the same place but in Martins present. He opened the portal. Cursing himself for not checking first he quickly shut the portal down as filth and water poured into the studio. Putting his bag of clothes on a high shelf he divested himself of his "costume" and draped himself in Martin's old and holey robe. With mop and bucket he cleaned up the mess. Both doors were opened as it was a warm day since the stench was making him ill, plus it would dry things up quicker. When all was as clean and fresh as he could make it, he reentered the position and date, did an eyes on and then repositioned the portal to open without flooding.

Redressed in renaissance high fashion he checked the area above ground and climbed out.

Walking to the Monastery/Hospital he pulled on the large door and entered into the courtyard. To his right was the fountain and, in an alcove next to it, was the sculpture. A nun, seeing his eyes roving over the facility, offered to show him around. The hospital was a long two storied building with the court open onto a garden. He recognized patches of flowers that he had seen in the sculpture. The nun explained that they compounded their own cures in the pharmacopeia.

On benches near the walls patients who were not confined to bed were getting air and sunlight. A Doctor was making his rounds and saluted the nun and her guest. Passing doorways, he saw beds where those who were extremely sick were restricted. From the coughs it sounded as if quite a few had consumption or tuberculosis. There were five wards where patients stayed. The rear of the building held the doctor's office, the pharmacopeia, a kitchen and a small library. Upstairs was a larger library, a scriptorium, and an open space for living. A small kitchen was also in place strictly to feed the monks and nuns. He was amused to see that the Nun's sleeping quarters were guarded by a locked gate while the monks had no such safeguards. It made him wonder who was being protected.

Arthur was relieved when they eventually returned to the fountain. She gave the fountain a short discourse but then showed off their beautiful sculpture. "It is called "The Nurse" and was commissioned by the doctor that has spoken to us." She touched it with pride and allowed her guest to gaze his fill. "The artist is a friend of Michelangelo and though not famous will make his mark soon. We are honored that he presented this to us at no cost." Arthur was in awe of the painted marble. The colors were true to life and the lovely, sculpted nurse looked out joyfully. The eyes sparkled with merriment and were so craftily sculpted that they were looking directly at you from any angle. He admired the statue at length while the nun waited patiently, her hands deep in the pockets of her dress. Realizing the nun might want to get back to her duties he thanked her and gave a ruby as a token of appreciation. As she ushered him out, he asked if she might know where he could find the sculpture as he had a commission for him. She etched out directions on a scrap of pottery and pointed him down the road.

The directions took him to a large square two storied building broken into apartments. He walked around trying to locate where Martin might reside. The difficulty was that few doorways announced who lived within. Finding an alley, he walked through to a colorful gardened court. The sounds of bees working amongst the flowers filled the air. Birds in the branches of a cherry laurel sang out lustily. He noticed a woven straw hat wandering low to the ground amongst the flowers. Making his way on an intercept course he found that underneath the hat was a very enchanting lady. "My apologies for disturbing you, but I am looking for an artist who I am informed lives in one of these apartments." She leapt to her feet. Grabbing his arm, she practically dragged him in her wake speeding up the stairs to the second floor. Hammering on the door the knocks were loud enough to wake the soundest sleeper.

Martin opened the door while wiping a cloth over his face. It appeared that he had just finished his morning ablutions and was setting the table for breakfast. The sight of Arthur dressed as a renaissance noble made him shout out with laughter. Pulling him in over the threshold and embracing him, slapped him on the back. Arthur's entrance into the apartment was assisted by Catarina who pushed from behind. "Catarina, please allow me to introduce my oldest friend, Arturo!" She dropped into a graceful curtsey and pulled out a chair for him at the table. Adding another plate to the table, they all sat down to breakfast. A loaf of bread graced the center of the table with a bowl of butter nearby, another bowl contained fruit. "It's a meager thing to offer a guest but later today I'll take you out later for a proper meal." Martin promised.

Arthur shrugged and helped himself to a plum and more bread. He found having wine with his breakfast disconcerting but when in Rome as they say. Catarina ate quickly and apologized but she had to get to the hospital for her morning shift. Martin and she went outside to say their intimate goodbyes. When Martin came back Arthur slouched comfortably in his chair and was admiring the sketches tacked to the wall. Drawings, paintings and models of Catarina were everywhere. "Seems she's gotten under your skin pal." Martin agreed. "She's inspired me into some of my best works so far. Later I'll take you to the Hospital and show you.." Arthur held up a hand, "Been there and seen it." "How the hell did you know about it?" Arthur pulled a picture from his pouch. It was the sculpture sans paint that was in the rear of the gallery.

Martin turned pale as the thought that his sculpture was now at Arthur's gallery almost 700 years from now. Arthur sat him down as he was beginning to sway on his feet. "Pal, I came down to see what your sculpture looked like when it was new.

I've been given three months to study it. A great deal of what I can and will say about it depends on what your plans are. Are you coming home or are you already home."

DUPLICITY

Martin looked around the apartment. He had gotten so set in his ways, that this life he was living now seemed more real than the life he had left behind. Since he never used it he had almost forgotten about his own portal. His drawings and sketches filled one of the walls, his recent small sculpture was in a corner while another larger one was in the corner of Michelangelo's studio. A painting of the garden and Catarina having lunch under the shade of the tree adorned the easel destined for a customer who had seen his sculpture. The day before he had been commissioned for several smaller sculptures and two frescos. These were destined for shops and pubs. Here he was able to be the artist he had considered himself. He was a classicist amongst the others of his ilk.

He was making a good living as an artist, and it fulfilled him. He had someone whom he cherished and who returned his love. What more did he have in the future that could compete with these. Still, it might be just as well to revisit his old life and then determine. "Tell you what, I can come home, or rather back there, tonight before Catarina comes home and yet be gone a week, month whatever it takes." He turned and was about to open his portal when he changed his mind. "Let's use your portal so I don't have to leave mine open. If Catarina saw it, it could lead to a lot of difficult explanations."

Getting into the sewer that late in the morning was difficult as people were all around. Martin whispered in Arthur's ear a plan he had. It was from a game they used to play as children. Arthur nodded his understanding and moved to a point forward and quite a bit away from the manhole. There he appeared to be looking on the roof of a nearby building. Martin walked alongside and Arthur grabbed his arm and pointed agitatedly at the roof. Martin also became visibly nervous and pointed and gesticulated with concern.

People stopped and peered across the road to see what was bothering the pair. They stopped others and asked what they could see. Martin and Arthur were gathering a large crowd and moving people in front of themselves. By getting them involved, they in turn brought others. Stealthily and quietly, they ducked into the crowd and made their way to the rear of the enlarging group of people. The way to the sewer was clear. They dropped down into the sewer unnoticed. Before diving beneath the street Martin had a last look at the still growing crowd and chuckled to himself, some gags work no matter where or when. He slid down the ladder and swung into his studio, home at last.

Martin and Arthur drank a toast then changed into more appropriate clothing. Seated in the Bentley's luxurious interior Arthur took the long way to the gallery. He wanted to approach it head on for the most startling view. The new look took Martin's breath away. What had been a large gallery had expanded into one three storefronts wide. On either side of the original gallery were separate frontages, one for local artists and the other for more exotic pieces. The center was reserved for the costliest pieces. Walking into the center Martin recognized the picture under a glass enclosure as a Van Gogh. It was one he had never seen before but the artist's signature was in the style. No actual signature was needed. Across was a Monet also secured behind glass. In the corners were several of his own pieces. It gave him a feeling of glory for his works to be in the company of Van Gogh and Monet.

In his office Arthur sat his friend on the couch and offered him a fine cigar. Martin accepted the cigar and offered his praise of the changes, "Looks like things are looking up around here. I'm impressed!" Arthur sat behind his desk and lit the cigar carefully. "Yep, it's finally becoming the place I always envisioned. Some early works by some of the most famous artists have come and gone through this gallery and it seems there are plenty more to come. All legitimate and with plenty of paperwork to verify their validity. I'm even making money on the writeups that I do regarding their history. I almost forgot, come down the back stairs and you can see what 700 years can do to a sculpture."

Stepping lightly down the stairs they arrived at the rear of the gallery where larger items were kept. Marta had all the lights on and had contrived to raise the statue onto rollers. She was turning it to get the best play of light and shadows so she could take more pictures. On a table nearby was a notepad and color wheel. "I've found more traces of colors and have written down what they were and where. Can I have your permission to colorize some of these and see if we can show what it looked like in full color?" Martin was amused by her enthusiasm. Arthur gave her the go ahead. She said she was going to practice on one of the sculptures Martin had in the gallery since those were simpler.

Martin carefully looked over the sculpture seeking any damage. At first, he noticed nothing but the missing paint. On closer inspection he noticed chips from when the roof caved in. The alcove had protected it for the most part and the damage was surprisingly minimal. Overcome with emotion he sat at the base and looked up into Catarina's marble face. He felt the distance between them, and it constricted his heart. He stood and kissed the cold lips then turned away. Walking up to Arthurs office it was as if he had aged thirty years since walking down.

Martin sagged in the chair unable to return to his normal cheerful self. "Arthur, congratulations on things going so well for you. I'm proud you still consider my works worthy of a place in the new setup. I'm feeling exhausted though. I'm gonna head out and go back to the studio." Arthur put an arm around his shoulder and walked him to the car. He held the door open and waited for Martin to slip inside. Instead Martin shook Arthurs hand and walked away. Arthur considered this change in his friend as temporary. "He just needs some time to reacquaint himself. He'll be back to his old self in no time." Closing and locking the car he strode around the studio and talked to customers. Later he would work on the packages for the next "find" of great works of the masters.

Martin breathed the fresh air lightly scented with the slightly fishy smells of Lake Michigan close by. Strolling along with hands in his pocket he made his way to the studio. Passing the pub he decided a beer and wings might perk him up. He placed his order at the bar, found an empty table, then just looked over the place. The place looked much the same as the last time he'd been there. Margaret was still seated next to a statue he had done of her as a drunken barfly. She always sat close so people would remark about the similarity and usually buy her a drink. When the food arrived, he ate slowly savoring the spicy wings and washing them down with long draughts of the bitter beer. After the fourth beer he felt calmer, almost sleepy but not quite ready for bed. He felt relaxed. Paying his bill, he headed for his studio home.

In the studio he tidied up a bit and looked over some of the pieces on the shelves. Most were early works and certainly not his best. One thing they all had in common was the small bird etched or painted somewhere on them. Even the work he was doing now contained it. He curled up on his cot and slept.

Two in the morning saw him wide awake and in a panic. All his works contained the bird, including his sculptures in the gallery! Swiftly he got dressed and started running to Arthur's apartment. Arriving in minutes he frantically pounded on the door. The sleepy and more than slightly irritated person who opened it was not Arthur. Apparently, Arthur had moved, and he didn't know where. He'd have to wait to see him later when the gallery opened.

Arriving home, he tried to work out a solution to the problem. It might be taken as a coincidence that two artists used the same symbol since he was known as Martino in Italy. He might have to change the style of the bird a little for when he went back in time. Either that or his future self would be considered a fraud who had copied the style of a renaissance artist. He made a strong pot of coffee to clear his head. Cup in hand he went to the window and sat cross legged on the riser.

Watching the world waken he peered upwards as dawn broke. The golden shafts of sunlight began to pierce the grey clouds low on the horizon. Driving slowly, several cars approached and turned towards the lake, fishermen on the way to catch some perch or trout while the lake was clear. Children filing past the window waved to him as they headed to the school down the street. Passing by with his keys in his hand the manager of the Dry Cleaners was opening early. Martin leaned back against the wall and waited.

Setting his now cold coffee aside he made himself presentable and headed to the gallery. By now the back door would be open and he could visit Arthur unseen. Passing a bakery, he acquired some rolls and coffees. It might be a good idea to sweeten Arthur up a little. He wasn't sure how he was going to take what he had to say.

Arthur and Marta were seated at the desk discussing changes to the gallery exhibits. In her hand Marta clutched a thumb drive she was anxious to show him. Martin knocked and entered. Realizing he was interrupting their meeting he apologized and was about to wait outside the door when Marta rose and brought him inside. "I'm glad you're here, what I wanted to show Arthur will be of interest to you too." She placed a large laptop onto the desk. Her hand was shaking so much with excitement that she could barely plugging the thumb drive in. She loaded up a split screen, one was Martins sculpture from the front of the gallery, the other was the sculpture from Italy. Both pictures had been colorized and were able to be rotated on the screen. Arthur rolled his chair into a better position and had Marta project what was on her screen onto the large wall tv. On the larger screen they could see the details better. Martin and Arthur looked at each other in wonder. Marta had gotten the colorization of the sculpture from Italy perfect.

She showed off her test of the colorization of Martins sculpture from the gallery. "O.K., now that I have your attention, I have a strange coincidence that I wanted to show you." She pointed at the nurse sculpture. I want to draw your attention to the small bird here." She pointed with a pen at the bird. "This bird is out of place and therefore has some significance. It is a Martin and I can believe it has some connection to the unknown sculpture." She then pulled up the sculpture that was in the front of the gallery. She rotated it until the back was facing them, she lowered the view and magnified it. Carved in relief was a small house martin with its beak open. She closed the picture then placed two more pictures on the split screen. One was a painting Martin had done of a woman by a lake picnicking under a tree. In the distance was a golden sunset reflecting off the river. In the tree was a martin singing its little heart out. It was almost identical to the Martin on the Italian sculpture.

What I don't understand is that if this sculpture is over 700 years old how does it have a bird that so closely resembles the one Martin uses as his signature. She looked at both men interrogatively. Martin seemed unable or unwilling to offer a comment. Arthur walked up to the screen and examined both pictures. "There are definite similarities, I can well understand your curiosity regarding this. Amazing really." He was becoming smoother as he went on. "Since male martins are usually all blue and black the resemblance in color is understandable." He turned to Martin, "Why do all of your birds have their beaks open?" Martin shrugged, "To show action, to make them seem more alive." Arthur did a google search for paintings of birds. Most were shown in song. "Again, the beak open seems to be prevalent in the majority of pictures. While it is an interesting coincidence, I believe it to be just that."

He turned to Marta with a grin, "Unless your conjecture is that our friend here is Methuselah who has been painting for eons." She turned off the computer. Arthur's answers had the ring of truth. She took up her notepad and excused herself telling Arthur that she would get the moves accomplished before noon. She had cleared a space on the main floor between Martins two statues for the Italian one. The colorized pictures would be on a pedestal nearby.

After she left Arthur held up a hand and went to check the door to ensure they had privacy. Martin laid out the pastries and congratulated him on how he handled Marta's concerns. Arthur grabbed a few kolaczki and coffee, Martin took a Bismarck. "You handled that real smooth Arthur." Martin bit into his doughnut sending custard dripping into his lap. Arthur handed over some napkins. "She'll be satisfied with the explanation. In fact, I may want to put out a writeup on it. Something about how prevalent certain items in past and present artworks are. Just in case the question comes up again. Oh, I need to know what your plans are. Are you going to stay here or go back to then. Like I said, a lot depends on your answer.

Martin licked his fingers and went to the bathroom to clean up. Sitting back down he considered his future. He slumped deep in thought weighing the merits of time and place. After a while he raised his head with a look of a determined man. "I am going home." Arthur leaned back puzzled. "You're going back to the studio? You're staying here?" Martin shook his head. "No, I mean home with Catarina. I can be me there. I can paint and sculpt to my heart's content, and I am making enough money at it. You know this is what

I've always wanted. Who knows, you may be right, my classical sculptures may be valuable now." Let me know if they ever come into their own."

Standing he shook Arthur's hand. Leaving out the back door he walked solemnly back to his studio. As suddenly as his solemn mood overcame him it just as suddenly dissipated. Realization came to him not of what he was leaving but of what he was going to. His future was in the past!

Rushing to arrive home he skidded to a halt when he saw Marta waiting at the doorway. She must have been there a while because she had gotten halfway down an ice cream cone from the Baskin Robins at the corner. He hesitated; he was anxious to go home but if Marta was here, she probably had information he ought to know about.

Ushering her inside he turned on the lights. She walked over to his holographic table and looked with curiosity at the jumble of mirrors, glass and lasers. She shook her head. It wasn't something Arthur was likely to be interested in. It was so jumbled, even Jackson Pollock would have a hard time understanding this thing. She turned and saw that Martin was waiting impatiently and the impatience wasn't masked very well. She sat at the desk and looked at Martin with frustration.

"Who are you, and how have you been around for over seven hundred years?"

TREACHERY

Martin's mouth opened. Then closed. She leaned back in the chair obviously more relaxed than he was. "I've worked with Arthur for seven years now. As the artist with the greatest salability when you produce your wonderful mechanical art he has taken you under his wing." She hooked a thumb at the portal projector/time machine. "Oh, I wouldn't give much hope for that thing, it's far too complicated." Martin relaxed a little. "All the time I have carefully examined your classical studies. Arthur prefers the Avant Garde because that sells for a high price, I am interested in the classics because of their artistic qualities. I have noticed certain traits in your works that would only be apparent to someone who really studied them. I noticed the same traits in the work we received from Italy. That one is over seven hundred years old, but the same traits are there." She folded her arms and waited.

Martin considered his options. He had been raised to be honest and after all this time he had rarely strayed off the path, when he did it was obvious. He just wasn't good at it. If he tried to lie to Marta, she would see it in his face for sure. If he was honest, it might lead to major consequences if he couldn't trust her. She could see his hesitancy and tried to reassure him. "Martin, I'm not sure what's going through your mind, but you can trust me. You won't believe this, but Arthur is the one you shouldn't be trusting."

From her pocket she pulled out a photocopy of a page from the Gallery ledger. It was for the sale of one of Martins pieces, the living head. It had sold for ten thousand dollars. Martin rummaged in his desk; he had a receipt from Arthur from the sale. Receipt from sale of artwork "Living Face" Sale Price $5.000.00 minus Commission to Gallery of 15% at $750.00 remainder $4,250.00 to Martin. He had gotten less than half the value and Arthur had still taken commission on what little he had received! Rage simmered inside him. No wonder he was just scraping by. If Arthur had cut all his sales in half and still charged commission, then he would be owed a hell of a lot of money.

"Martin he's been pricing your works very high or auctioning some of the best. I only realized yesterday when I saw one of the check stubs that you were being royally cheated. Frankly, it's your own fault for not taking more interest. I guess I really should be surprised though, most artists aren't concerned about the money, just art. Here's what I came to discuss with you. Arthur has been discovering a lot of early works from the masters recently. His first find was a Van Gogh, then a Monet, a Degauss and lots of others. Most are being auctioned and are netting him millions. I'll admit that some of that money has gone into expanding and reconditioning the Gallery. What's odd is that he has a paper trail on all the works, but when I looked up the galleries and collectors from the papers, there weren't any with those names. Martin, those pages are all aged and seem to be genuine, but I don't believe in them. I can't figure it out. Now a sculpture comes in for evaluation from Italy that has all the hallmarks of your works. I ask you again, what the hell is going on!"

Martin walked around the studio debating what to say. He had just been told that he had been cheated by someone who he had considered his best and practically only friend. Now

Marta had come along, showed him her discoveries, described Arthur's duplicity and deceit, and showed him how he and his portal were being used so Arthur could not only enrich himself but pass himself off as an expert on early works of the masters. Every rule he had set up for this thing he had created was being ignored.

He turned to Marta, "how well do you speak Italian?" The question took her by surprise. "I speak a bit, I was learning it because you and Arthur talk in it when you don't want me to hear what you're talking about." Martin grinned and took her to a costumer to see about fitting her for the renaissance. When they emerged, they went back to the studio taking the long way. Martin had an urge for pastrami and rye and there was only one place that did it right. Passing the Under the El Deli they stopped in to get a quick lunch. Sated and in a much better mood now they went to the studio, changed and Martin fired up the portal.

Marta was in shock as she saw the mass of mirrors, lasers, and glass plates coming alive and projecting what looked like the underside of a sewer. "Martin walked through and grabbed hold of the ladder on the left." He motioned for Marta to follow. Stark terror showed on her face as she realized she was going back in time hundreds of years. In a moment she calmed down, "well," she thought, "if both Martin and Arthur have been doing it, so could she." She stepped through and Martin assisted her in grasping the ladder. Peering out of the sewer he waited until it was clear enough that they could emerge safely.

Martin allowed her time to get her composure and bearings. She looked around her admiring the statues that stood in front of shops and in alcoves of the front walls. Frescos adorned the inside walls of shops and pubs. Art was everywhere and for someone who loved classical art she was in heaven. She started walking, not really sure where she was headed but allowing inspiration to lead her on. From a corner she heard loud banging, hammering and the sound of large chunks falling. Martin took her arm and led her across the street to where Michelangelo had his studio. He didn't tell her whose studio it was. He felt it would be more fun to see if she recognized Michelangelo from his portraits.

Peeking inside she was surprised when Martin opened the door and saluted Michelangelo with a "Good morning Maestro". He led her to the corner he used and showed her his latest work. It was of a woman standing with arms forward slightly bent and hands clasped. The dress she wore was laying in folds along the contours of her body. The beautiful face looked out with a beneficent expression. It was the face of an impassioned saint. The muscles that showed were defined but supple. The hair was luxurious and hung low down her back and front. Marta stood staring in wonder as the sculpture captured and held her. She closed her eyes so the image would be ingrained in her memory. "It's beautiful!" She exclaimed.

A gravelly voice from her left, "It is good yes?" She looked over into a face vaguely familiar. She opened her mouth to speak but nothing came out. She peered intently at a face she was sure she knew. "Michelangelo?" she inquired. "But of course! What do you think though of our friends work here." He went over to Martin and placed an arm around his shoulder. "He has talent this one. He has the vision and can see it in the marble and release the image! He can bring it out in paint. Once he has developed his talents, he will be a master!

Marta was about to exclaim that Martin was one already but felt Martin squeeze her elbow and realized one does not contradict Michelangelo. She agreed that there was indeed potential in Martins' work. Michelangelo took her by the elbow and led her to his latest sculpture. "Look on a masters work." He showed the image with undisguised pride. The sculpture was of a woman also, but she must have been an amazon. The muscles large and so well defined, she felt it was as if he had sculpted Hercules and then at the last moment changed his mind and added boobs. She looked from Martins to Michelangelo's sculptures and internally decided she preferred Martins. She professed her admiration of Michelangelo's work and with his permission reached out to touch it. He glowed with satisfaction at her adulation. Pointing a finger at Martins sculpture he remarked, "this one will go into the Sistine Chapel just as my works are." He nudged Martin, "My work is closer to God though." He escorted them to the door and invited her to return any time with or without Martin.

Outside she laughed and shook her head. "Such an ego that one. I guess he has earned it but whew, I'd hate to get into a scrap with the kind of females he sculpts." Her mind cast back to Martins sculpture. "I can't get over the beauty of the sculpture you created. It's so different from the ones in the gallery. This one has passion and a look of adoration. It grabs you and holds you, that's for sure. The face is familiar too. Is she the same as the one from the hospital." Martin nodded as he led her to the stalls.

He changed out a small jewel for enough to get her whatever she wanted. He just hoped she didn't want too much.

What she wanted was a fresco. Down a side street they found an artist block. Here were artists with their products held up with stones or twigs. Not famous artists but their works were good enough to be desired. Martin greeted several as if he had known them. They called him Maestro and he apparently had been helping them, some with money, some with instruction and some with praise. From their welcome he was well liked and they sat for a while amongst them passing wine around and talking.

As they drank and talked, Marta walked around admiring the works. She found several small paintings that she wanted, one fresco and a couple of statues. Martin paid royally for what she wanted giving more then was asked for. The works were tied up and made easy for transport then passed on to a carter who would deliver them to his apartment. "They'll be waiting outside the door when we get there." Amongst the stalls she was transfixed by an intricately woven tapestry. She was holding it in the light and contemplating asking Martin to buy it for her when a screech split the air.

Martin whipped around and saw a basket flung in the air scattering fruit, fish and odds and ends far and wide. The screech had come from Catarina who had spied Martin with Marta and was running, practically flying in their direction. The look of jealous rage on Catarina's face was terrifying and Martin placed himself between Catarina and Marta.

Capturing Catarina in his arms he had a difficult time holding on to her. Lashing out claws she was a wildcat in fiercest fight. She kicked, clawed, and while Marta wasn't completely fluent in Italian she knew enough to know she was getting the biggest cursing of her life. Marta hastened to explain that she did not have designs on Martin but couldn't make herself understood over Catarina rage.

Martin placed his hand over Catarina's mouth and was promptly bitten. She turned her venom on him and he was scratched on the side of his face. While Catarina's focus was turned on Martin, Marta ducked aside, collected a jug and went to the fountain. Filling it quickly she darted back and poured it over Catarina and Martin. The crowd that had formed at the first screech roared with laughter and applauded. Catarina spluttered and would have spun and attacked Marta except in the momentary onslaught Martin took Catarina in his arms and kissed her so long and passionately that Catarina melted and returned his kiss to the applause of the detaching crowd. Marta watching them so lovingly intimate she was close to becoming irrationally jealous herself.

Once separated Martin introduced Marta and explained that she was an acquaintance through his business partner in another town. She had come to visit and do some shopping before heading home. Catarina apologized for incivility and scurried back to pick up her strewn belongings. As they started to walk to the apartment the man who was selling the tapestry approached with it offering it at a lower price. Martin handed over the sum requested. Marta rejoiced holding her prize close to her. Passing amongst the stalls that were on the way to the apartment Catarina augmented her supplies adding enough for the three of them. Martin added several loaves of bread and a bottle of wine. Marta was surprised to see that the wine came in half gallon bottles that were wrapped with straw from base to top.

Seated at the table Marta occupied herself watching Martin and Catarina preparing lunch. She was amused to see the division of labor. Catarina did the prep work while Martin did the cooking. Everything was put into the skillet at specific times to ensure everything came out cooked together. As they cooked, they talked and teased each other. It was a side of Martin she never imagined.

The apartment was compact but comfortable. Sketches and wax models were on shelves around the room. Canvas stacked on the floor or leaning against the wall. There were some models that Catarina must have been doing and looking from one to the other she could see the improvements.

Over fish stew Marta complemented Catarina regarding her art works. Catarina inclined her head in appreciation of the complement, "I am not so good as Martino, but who knows, someday my works will be famous too. In the meantime, I am famous because of his sculptures and paintings. She straightened proudly. "Has he shown you his latest? It is in Michelangelo's studio." "He has and it is, I do not have the words for how beautiful it is." Here she decided to get in Catarina's good graces by stating, "But then, all he did was capture the beauty before him." Catarina blushed and thanked Marta for her kindness.

Catarina asked if she would be staying long. Marta replied that she had to go home as her husband would be anxious if she was away long. "I was sent here to take care of some business for Arturo, when I saw our friend he recognized me and was gracious enough to escort me." Catarina wrapped Martins arm in hers. "You must escort her to the carriage, you will not allow her to carry these by herself, will you?" She waived a hand at the purchases Marta had made. Martin promised he would take care of it.

A monk knocked at the door requesting to see Catarina, "My apologies but you are needed at the hospital. We have soldiers who are arriving in need of care and the doctor has asked for everyone to assist." He took off at a run to return to the hospital yelling for Catarina to hurry. Catarina stomped as she put on her apron and cap. "It is my day off and it is not fair. I worked all last night and now I have to go back." Martin assisted her to tie the apron, "I will send Marta off and then I will come to the hospital and assist too. I don't have your knowledge, but I can do what I can to help. We can at least be together that way." Catarina kissed him and then sped out the door, coming back suddenly she kissed Marta as a friend and begged her to come back when they could spend time together. "I will send Martino on an errand or something and we can have time just for us." She giggled and twirled then ran down the steps and was lost in the distance within moments.

"Well, let's get you home now." Marta looked about at her purchases and grimaced. "I'm not looking forward to trying to bring these things threw the sewer." Martin started opening the easel converting it into a portal. "What's your address and we'll put them directly into your living room." She gave it and her eyes popped when she saw a window appear and she was looking inside her apartment. She went through and Martin handed her the pictures and tapestry. She stepped back through and gave Martin a peck on the cheek. The portal closed with her waving goodbye. Martin began to convert the portal back to an easel. A thud made him turn around and the sight of Catarina slumped on the floor her face cold and pale made him shudder. He carried her to the bed and cared for her as best he could. When her eyes fluttered open she looked over to where the easel was still partially converted and the paint box open revealing the laptop.

She sat up and swinging her legs over the bedside endeavored to rise with Martin attempting to have her lay down. Unfortunately, she had seen too much. He realized he had a great deal of explaining to do. Rubbing his temples, he poured out some wine but wished he had something much stronger.

EXEGESIS

Catarina looked over the easel and pulled in and out the mirrors and pieces of glass. She found the cord traveling to the pots. Martin stopped her before she got a shock from touching the copper posts. She looked at the laptop and pushed a few buttons without understanding what she was seeing and what it was doing. She turned slowly around and sitting at the table waited patiently for an explanation. Martin sat opposite her and looked into her eyes. It took a moment before he found something to say. "Shouldn't you be at the hospital?" His head rang from a stinging smack upside his head. "Sorry Catarina, I'm just not sure how to explain all this."

He rose and went over to begin activating the portal. "I guess the only way to explain it is to show you." He reopened all the slots and then just as suddenly jumped to the door locking it and closing the drapes over the windows. Catarina was impressed with all the secrecy but thought if he had used as much before they wouldn't be where they are now. She tried to picture what would have happened if she had returned to find closed curtains and a locked door especially if voices had been heard inside. What she had done at the market would have been nothing compared to what she would have done then.

"Catarina, come here please." She approached slowly unsure of what was going on. He pointed to each piece in turn. Starting with the birdcage he started his explanation. "This provides energy to the pots, the pots provide energy to my, well just think of this as a really fast abacus. It can figure out things by itself." He turned on everything and as it booted up, he explained further. "When all these things are put together, they allow me to move in time. I could be here now and travel to yesterday or tomorrow.

He paused and thought about the things Marta had said. He needed to safeguard his unit and he couldn't do it here. He needed a place to store it that would be safe, secure and unknown to anyone but them. "Catarina, I need to go and find a studio where we can store this. It isn't safe here and I can't take any chances." Catarina looked the machine over. "My apartment." She looked to see if Martin approved. The grin on his face made her proud. "Always the brilliant one, don't you get tired of being so clever." She rose and after kissing Martin began to carry the smaller articles down to the apartment. When all was arranged and secured Martin looked more confident. He reactivated the portal and explained their next move.

I am telling the computer to take me to where I lived before I met you." As the computer activated and Realtime projected into the easel, Catarina saw darkness in which shelves, a door and window were just barely visible. "In the place you see, is the original of this machine. It allowed me to travel and thankfully to meet you. I want you to see the world I lived in." She put her hand through and felt the cold. She put one foot through and stood in two times. "We can come back?" Martin nodded. With the faith of trust and love she stepped through without a qualm. Martin saw her go towards the door, turn and wait for him to join her.

He entered his studio and turned on the desk lamp. He fired up the original portal and programed it for the return trip. Projected in the studio Catarina saw their apartment and within the apartment the easel showing a lighted studio inside the frame. Martin walked into the past, marched forward through the easel and into the present. Catarina did the same. Once assured that she could get back home she went over to Martins cot and sat down. Martin closed the portals and then joined her. "Darling we can go home anytime you want but I want to show you around a bit." He looked over at a clock on the shelf. It was 0300. He hadn't wanted to arrive later but now that he was here he opened the portal and set it for 0800. Taking her hand they walked through into a studio that was well lit. Sunshine was filtering through the morning fog and it promised to be a warm and sunny day.

Catarina had to sit down again. Martin rummaged through his clothes looking for something he could dress her in. He chose a pair of dress pants and one of his few decent shirts. She was embarrassed when she came out of the bathroom but gained courage from Martins embrace. Martin changed, closed off the portal and checked the front door. Satisfied, he found his wallet and keys then walked out the back door. Through the alley and around the corner they entered a small diner and ordered breakfast. Catarina might not have been able to read the menu but she could understand some of the pictures. So much being available for breakfast confused her. She pointed to what she felt she could eat. When it arrived, it was clear she wasn't going to be able to eat much. Martin also ate sparingly. He had gotten used to a different way of eating and the food wasn't what he wanted. He received the check and paid it by leaving the money on the table. At the exit Catarina handed him the money, explaining he had forgotten it. She was surprised when he returned it to the table but decided not to say anything.

Back on the streets they walked to the Gallery. The sights and sounds were overwhelming to Catarina. He was holding her close and could feel her trembling. The closest she came to something familiar was a farmers' market in a parking lot. She rushed inside and wandered around the stalls. Buying things at random gave her a feeling of security, it was familiar, it served to calm her. A block later they were at the Gallery. She could understand some of the pictures and wandered around aimlessly. From the door leading to the stairway to Arthur's office came a shout of delight. "Catarina!" Marta ran over and hugged her friend. Martin followed as Marta showed Catarina around. Only as they neared the rear of the gallery did Catarina see the large sculpture that had once graced the hospital. Stumbling with emotion she walked over. A guard was not going to let her get near it but at a sign from Marta he unlatched the rope.

Catarina had seen it unpainted so was able to recognize it. She ran her hands over the chipped portions on the hands and back. She looked into the face and was relieved it wasn't chipped or marred. When she looked back at Marta and Martin she had tears in her eyes. It felt like every chip was a piece out of her heart. The tears momentarily blinded her. Martin led her up the stairs and into Arthur's office. Laying on the couch she slowly recovered. Marta helped herself to a shot of scotch, she felt she needed it after the shock of seeing Catrina. Martin kneeled beside Catarina and stroked her hair and spoke soothing words.

Arthur walked in with a picture wrapped in cloth. At the sight of everyone in his office he almost dropped the picture. Backing up he was about to walk back out, instead he paused at the door. "Uh, hello all, give me a moment and I'll be right with you." He disappeared into the bathroom emerging moments later sans picture. Drying his hands as he entered the room once more, he was wearing his most debonair expression. Seated on the edge of the desk he looked with concern at Catarina. Marta hastened to explain their presence. "I was showing Catarina around and she saw Martins sculpture, she became upset at the damage. I brought her up here so she wouldn't upset the customers and staff."

Arthur was most sympathetic. "Of course, you couldn't have done anything else." He turned to Catarina who was now sitting up. "Feeling better, that's good. I'd love to have you stay and chat but I have a very busy schedule. He ushered them to the door like a mother hen with her chicks. "Please call me next time and we'll have lunch or something." The door closed swiftly, and they could hear the locks slam.

Marta cast a look at Martin. He understood perfectly and was going to find out what Arthur had been up to. "I'll let you know what I find out." "I'll report what I find on this end. Can I stop by the studio later?" Martin nodded and walked out the back door with Catarina. Walking back to the studio Catarina placed her arm around Martins waste and pulled his arm around her. She could feel his muscles tight under his shirt. Tenseness seemed to exude through every pore. "This Arturo, he has made you angry." It wasn't a question but a statement of fact. He is no longer your friend?"

Martin stopped walking and held her close. His world made no sense. A man who he had considered as his one true friend had betrayed him. He had been betraying him for a long time apparently. Martin felt not only betrayed but used. He was determined to do what he could to stop Arthur from acquiring any more works of art through his machine. The problem was without the time machine he couldn't get himself and Catarina home. The thought of sending her back home and destroying the unit did occur to him for a moment. Only for a moment though, the thought of being without her was a future he couldn't face.

In the studio he locked the door and closed the curtains. He sat down at his desk and did some deep thinking. Marta sat on the cot and waited. Martin looked around trying to figure a way to stop Arthur that wouldn't prevent him from traveling. There were other artists to learn from and places he always longed to see. From a side desk drawer he found the keyboard from his old computer. Why he kept it he didn't know but looking at it made him feel he was holding the answer. To the left and right sides were keys designated for a specific task, sound, internet, video, etc. it was even programable for adding specific commands. A slow smile spread over his lips. Specific commands would be a good start. He went to where he stored his clothes and found a wide belt. A spare laser pointer was found in the center drawer, battery pack, frame and mirrors. He laid out pieces as he found them. Firing up his computer he set about programing the keyboard for a stand alone control pad for linking to his laptop.

The keyboard programmed, he took it apart and placed the components onto the belt. Wide as the belt was it wasn't wide enough. He switched to a leather vest. It would be slightly cumbersome, but it would do for a start. Catarina watched as he drew outlines for each piece. From a mapping program he downloaded every map they had. Next was a program for GPS that could still track when no GPS was available. It worked off of the last position then adapted for direction and step rate using an internal compass. With everything laid out and marked he was ready to sew everything into the vest.

Marta watched his efforts with growing amusement. For a while she could contain her laughter but eventually it burst forth. She pulled Martin from the chair and sat down. "At art you are the master and I am the pupil, but at sewing you are merda and I am your master, mistress?" She pieced the first component in place and swiftly sewed it in. "Why don't you get us something to eat, make or get plenty in case Marta comes early." Martin scurried away admonishing her not to open the door for anyone but Marta.

Marta arrived soon after Martin left and was let in only after Catarina ensured she was alone. Marta walked to the desk with Catarina and sat on the chair opposite. "What is this?" She asked pointing to the odd vest. Catarina shrugged. "I don't know but it is something to do with Martino being angry with Arturo." Martin arrived with bags of groceries and set up several tv trays to have somewhere to prepare. Martin and Catarina changed jobs when she had put in the last stitch. Marta assisted Catarina and they softly chatted as they worked. Martin completed wiring and plugged in the batteries. He stepped into the bathroom and moments later he came back out smiling. Over the vest he placed a flannel shirt, it was large enough to hide the vest without looking odd.

Catarina called Martin over to get something to eat. They had sliced everything thinly and spread it out on a platter. A stack of Naan bread was at the side and Marta filled the bread with pieces of meat and vegetables, folded it in half and took a big bite. Catarina and Martin followed suit and talking was impossible as they feasted.

A gust of wind sent dust over the food as the door burst open and rebounded off the rubber wall plate. Arthur stood in the door his face a blank mask. Martin rose but sat back down when Arthur shook his head and pulled out the handle of a gun. Sliding it back into his pocket he had no need to pull it or aim it at any of them, the threat was understood.

"Sorry to disturb your meal." He looked over the spread. "Think I'll help myself too, please go on eating." He made himself a sandwich and strolled over to the portal. As he ate he turned it on and programmed it for Martin and Catarina's apartment. Arthur finished programming and eating at the same time. With the portal opened he stepped through. Looking around he searched for Martins unit. "What happened to the easel unit?" Martin looked forlorn, "It blew up. To much to ask of it off of battery power. I had the main unit here preprogramed for a few different days and times. I was going to set a new selection later this evening. It was the only way I could figure on getting back and forth." Arthur was scrutinizing Martins face and saw no deception there. For once Martin had been able to lie convincingly when it was needed most.

"Martin, I believe Marta has told you everything." Martin was about to deny this when Marta interceded. "Of course I did, He has a right to know you have been ripping him off."

Arthur pursed his lips. "Such devotion to our little buddy is touching. Since you prefer classical to Avant Garde, I think you might want to join Martin and Catarina. Marta made a dash for the back door. As fast as Arthur whipped the gun out Martin threw a sculpture distracting him. Marta couldn't get the door to unlock and looked back beaten.

"Nice try but when your beat it's best to accept it." He pointed the gun at them and motioned them through. As Martin passed him, he held him by the arm. "I just wanted to tell you that I've sold two of the classical sculptures that were on either side of the Italian one. Made a nice sale. He handed Martin an envelope. Five thousand in hundreds. Martin was about to throw the envelope in Arthur's face when Arthur stuffed it into Martins pocket and pushed him through. "Don't spend it all in one place," he admonished laughing as the portal turned black and closed.

RETRIBUTION

Martin walked through to find Marta lying on the bed crying. Catarina was doing her best to comfort her. "you're not trapped Marta; Martino's machine is still here." Marta sat up so suddenly it made her dizzy. "But Martin said it had burnt up or something." Catarina grinned, "Martino is not a good liar but he lied good this time." Martin pulled a mini keyboard from his pocket. Pushing a few buttons caused a portal to project in front of them leading into Marta's apartment. The look of relief on Marta's face was almost comical if it hadn't been so tragic. She leapt to her feet and was going to dash through when Martin shut the portal down before she reached it.

Marta gasped and looked accusingly at Martin. Martin intimated that she should sit. Catarina joined them at the table and poured out wine for all. Martin took off the shirt and vest. "Marta, I wanted to show you can go home and you can do so anytime. "I want to go home now!" She exclaimed. "I know Marta but please hear me out. You go home now and what? Go back to work at the gallery?" He cocked an ironical brow. She hesitated, took a drink of wine and waited to hear Martin out.

"Marta if you go home Arthur is going to want to know how. He was not hesitant to aim his gun at you when you tried to escape so I wouldn't want him to find you until were ready to offset any plans he might have." She agreed, though reluctantly. Catarina looked Marta over. "She can stay in my old apartment. She is almost like me so my clothes will fit. She can stay until we are ready." She looked at Marta hoping that her offer would be accepted. Marta reached over and hugged them both. "I guess you're right." Her smile faded as a new complication entered her thoughts." If I'm gone for a long time though I'll lose everything. My apartment, all my things, I'll have to start all over again." Martin did a bit of thinking. "What do you need to keep things in order?" "My tablet for a start, but without internet it's useless."

Martin opened the portal to her apartment again. "Get what you need including the tablet and some clothes, once you come back, we'll set about hiding you from the evil Arturo." Martin used the portal momentarily to change the money into jewelry and stones. When he returned the portal back to Marta's apartment she was sitting on her couch surrounded by bags and looking miserable. When the portal opened, she gave a scream of delight and tossed bags and items to Martin who handed them to Catarina, who placed them in a corner.

Marta and Catarina went down to check Catarina's former abode. While she was gone Martin went to the present but opened the portal into Wisconsin. He was taking no chances. He went to an electronic supply store and filled a trunk with anything and everything he could need to satisfy their wants. He was gone for only an hour, but in that time the ladies had moved Marta in and she was changed into one of Catarina's dresses. Martin sent the ladies out for the day with plenty of money and a few jewels in case they didn't have enough cash. With the apartment clear and quiet he set about creating a portal window for Marta's apartment. With that she could have internet. He left instructions on using the battery system so she could recharge her tablet.

The window was created and installed in an obscure area of Marta's temporary home. He decided to run some tests on a wearable portal window so he could carry the internet with him. If this succeeded he could wear the vest anywhere and anywhen and still come and go at his pleasure. After a few tries he discovered a four second lag time when out of the apartment. He tried several areas that offered a modicum of privacy, mostly bathrooms, and leapt into his studio at a past point where he knew neither he nor Arthur would be around.

He spent a few hours on his laptop loading a drop-down menu for places and times he could load into the vest. As long as the list wasn't extensive it would suffice. Now his biggest concern was power. How many trips could he do with one set of batteries. From out of the trunk, he pulled a laser pointer that most people would use for a cat. He wanted to see if this could produce the portal. Being smaller and cheaper on power, it would be preferable and might even mean less parts for the vest unit. A quick trip to his studio and he pulled out all the electronics books he had. While doing a survey of his former home he noticed that Arthur had changed the locks. A fat lot of good that would be against himself!

He fired up the computer. Taking a thumb drive, he downloaded all the trips Arthur had taken from first to the last one. He was getting an idea that would foil Arthur. He shut down the computer and was walking through the portal when he heard the front door being unlocked. He shut his portal down just as his foot crossed over the threshold.

When Catarina and Marta arrived, they did so empty handed but happy and slightly intoxicated. "Sorry to see you couldn't find anything you wanted." Both ladies burst into laughter. "Wait until you see, we had to send it on the carts" It was carts in the plural that made Martin shudder. He looked around the small place wondering where all they had bought would fit. "Catarina hugged Martin and seeing the look on his face reassured him that most would be going to Marta's apartment. He had Marta sit down and they held a council of war.

"Marta, I need to know where your allegiance lies." She sat straighter and leaning forward, she set Martin at ease. "Martin, He was using you and cheating only you. He has been using your machine only to enrich himself. He doesn't give a damn about anybody else. Once I saw that, I no longer took his side. Besides, the fact that the bastard took a pot shot at me. I'm on yours and Catarina's side." Catarina smiled and hugged Marta when she heard she was included.

"You two get your belongings situated, I have a little shopping to do of my own." He changed into a loose shirt and paint spattered pants. His feet stuck out of rope soled sandals. He pushed the keypad and walked through the portal. From where they sat Marta and Catarina saw he had not gone to the studio but to a dark cavernous area. Shrugging they anxiously peered out of the windows waiting for the carters to arrive.

Martin's first port of call was the same as Arthurs. He emerged from a shed and looked around. A great artist is not only conversant with his or her contemporaries but with those who came before. Martin recognized where and when he was. France during the time of Vincent Van Gogh. He stopped a passerby and asked for the abode of Van Gogh. He was corrected that while Van Gogh lived there the abode belonged to his friend. Accepting the correction, he made his way to the cottage.

From the doorway he looked across the lane to see what was shown in the painting, except he was seeing it in real life. He leaned against the door momentarily to steady himself. Van Gogh was an artist he greatly admired, and he was standing on his threshold. The door was opened by an elderly woman with a young boy clutching at her leg. He spoke in English then corrected to French. "Excuse me, is Mr. Van Gogh at home?" She ushered him inside as the boy ran off to tell his mother that company had arrived. The cottage was small and though not untidy was crowded. There were two beds at either corner in the rear, a small cooking range where a pot of soup was simmering and sending off fragment odors of meat and vegetables, A table laid for breakfast with a wine bottle centered and covered with a cloth. To the right and front in the illumination of two large windows were a couple of chairs and a small table.

The mother of the small boy was sewing a stuffed doll. She half rose as Arthur approached then resumed her sewing. The elderly lady seated Arthur in the empty chair and brought him a glass of wine. In a corner stood Van Gogh contemplating his next picture. The light streaming through the window fell onto a blank canvas. He began sketching the outline for his painting. On a stool stood the paints, pallet, and brushes at the ready. The lady put down her sewing and tapped Van Gogh on the shoulder whispering in his ear.

Van Gogh dropped the pencil on the stool, dusted himself down and approached Martin. Martin rose and held out his hand. Artist recognized artist and Van Gogh sat down to hear what Martin had come for. Martin had only worked out a rudimentary idea of what he was doing. Hoping that inspiration would fill in the rest he leaned back and began.

"Thank you for taking the time to talk with me. I would like to ask you to do something very unusual with me." Van Gogh raised an eyebrow at this odd request. Martin hastened to explain, "I have a friend who professes to be an art expert. I think he's full of shit and doesn't know good art from bad. He is coming to see you to try and get one of your paintings. He doesn't care about art, only money and thinks that a work of yours will be worth something in the future. I agree that your paintings are both unusual and unique. I appreciate that you are an artist for arts sake.

It is a difficult way of living when you care more for the art then money. I am one myself." His face grew angry, "That is why I am so upset with Arthur. He cares only about money and nothing about art. He really doesn't understand what he buys." Vincent's head sank into his chest. He nodded in agreement that a person like that was not worth knowing. When he looked up he had the inquisitive look of a man interested in another's idea. "What do you have in mind?" "I want you to let me do a picture in chalk, pen and paint. We'll place it amongst your other pictures and you offer it to him. I have seen enough of your pictures that I should be able to do a passable imitation for one as simple as this. If he recognizes it as a fake, we will know he actually knows something if not, then he is as stupid as he is wealthy and cares nothing for art and artists. He is just a greedy bastard."

Vincent took down the picture he was working on and placed a small canvas on the easel. Opening his case of paints and tools he made Arthur free to use whatever he needed.

Martin looked around for something to copy. Seeing the elder lady absorbed in her work he did a quick sketch. In order to accomplish a reasonable facsimile of a work by Van Gogh he needed to use the smooth strokes and lines Van Gogh used when working in this medium. Had he been doing an oil painting he would have used short strokes and daubs of paint indicating movement and depth. Van Gogh lounged on the bed and watched the painting take form. As it neared completion he rose and hovered behind Martin. "Where have you seen my works?" Martin was short by the abruptness of the question. "Your brother Theo has shown me some when I chanced on his Gallery." He was glad he was facing away from Vincent as it appalled him to have to lie.

Completed, the picture was hung on a wire to dry. Martin was invited to sit and join them for breakfast. Plates were distributed and all were served eggs on bread with dried cake called Rusks on the side. Martin added some cheese to his plate. Simple though the breakfast was it was excellent. Van Gogh ushered Martin outside to relax and smoke. They discussed many subjects including painting. When the talk drifted to Van Gogh's extended family Van Gogh tensed. He waited for a comment from Martin when informed that his companion was a prostitute.

He relaxed when all Martin said was that they seemed to be happy together and that she was an excellent cook. Martin rose and stretched intimating it was time to leave. Van Gogh rose also and shook his hand. "It will be interesting to see the outcome." He shook hands again with Martin and watched Martin wander down the road. Going into the house he checked the picture then placed it with a stack of others, smiling at the test they were about to do. He kissed them all then said he was going out for a walk and would be back soon.

Several hours later there was another knock at the door. Arthur had come to pay his respects.

TWO TO ONE

Martin returned in excellent humor. He sat at the table and laughed. His grand plan was beginning well. Once he developed everything to his satisfaction he could go forward and destroy the original portal. This would prevent Arthur from trying to change things back again. He was looking over the list of artists Arthur had visited when Catarina waltzed in. Stumbled in would have been more like it. Marta followed a bit more sober and trying to get Catarina to calm down. Seeing Martin Catarina flung herself into his arms. She rained kisses over him and squeezed him with all her might. When she squeezed Martin expelled air from his nether region which set Catarina into hysterics. Marta was apologizing for the state Catarina was in when the light was blocked, and a shadow extended inside. Turning towards the door the shadow joined to the form of a man and a very angry one at that.

Catarina's father strode into the room and stared in disbelief at the state his daughter was in. Marta seeing which way the wind was blowing edged herself around behind him and dashed out the door like any sensible person. Catarina slid off Martins lap and sat on the chair. The look on her father's face sobered her quicker than a pot of black coffee. He sat down hard onto the other chair. Catarina began, "Padre, I." That was as far as she got her father's raised hand silenced her effectively. Since entering he had glanced at Catarina then his unswerving look hovered on Martin. Without changing his line of sight he requested Catarina to return to her apartment. She slunk away casting an eloquent look of pity on Martin.

Without preamble or comment on Catarina's condition he launched into speech. "Martin, of the fact that my daughter is living in intimacy with you I say nothing. She is a woman grown and I have always allowed her to live as she sees fit. Of her love for you I also say nothing. Originally, I had someone in mind for her to marry but she had no desire to marry when the subject arose. The fact that since she has been with you, she has neglected her duties at the hospital, this I do have something to say. The fact that I see her in drink as I have never seen her I also have something to say. She is no longer a child and I do not treat her as one. But I am still her father and will ensure myself as to your intentions. Martin had never had a father ask his intentions towards their daughter before and he was almost embarrassed by the question.

He cleared his throat and tried to present an open, honest countenance to this man. "Sir, I hold your daughter close in my heart. She has been more than my muse who has guided me to my finest works, but she is also my life. It is my intention to ask her to be my wife, with your permission of course." Her father considered the man before him. As an artist his work was exemplary, as a man he was one whom he felt he could trust. "My concern is that as an artist will you be able to support a wife?" Martin went to a chest and pulled out two leather bags. The longer contained coins of high denominations he had been collecting since his arrival. The smaller contained jewels. He poured out the contents onto the table. "My works are selling, and I will make more." Her father was impressed, "and if your work ceases to sell or your patron relinquishes you?" Martin was relaxed and ready with an answer. "Even those who sweep the streets are paid, there is always work and work supports a wife and family."

Catarina's father rose and shaking Martins hand departed. Catarina watching from the window of her old apartment saw her father leave looking better pleased then when he had arrived. Whether that was a good thing for them or not remained to be seen. She stole up the steps as quietly as she could. Approaching the apartment from the right she leaned slightly so she could see inside. Martin was seated at the table and replacing money and jewels into their bags. "You are alright?" Martin chuckled at her trepidation. "He didn't try to kill me if that is what you're thinking, yes, everything is fine." She let out a shrill whistle which let Marta know the coast was clear. Marta came charging up the steps and burst into the room. Diving into a chair she was eager to hear what happened. Catarina came up behind Martin and hugged him then went to her own chair.

"So, when do you want to have the wedding?" Catarina was just about to sit when Martin asked the question. She was so shocked she missed the chair and flopped onto the floor. Martin jumped to his feet to assist her. Marta was no help as she was convulsed in laughter.

"Are you serious?" Catarina and Marta asked at once. Martin dropped to one knee and held out a ring he had kept out of the leather pouch. "Catarina, I'm asking you to marry me." Catarina was confused. She had just discovered that this man she loved was from somewhen very different from when and where she lived, could he really be happy living a life here or would she have to adapt to when he lived. A world so forcign that she would have nothing to cling to. A world so advanced she would not know how to do anything. She closed his fingers over the ring and to his surprise sat down on the chair. He rose and sat across from her bewildered. He put the ring on the table.

"Catarina, I think I understand your hesitancy, but I want you to tell me what you're thinking. I don't want to guess, and I don't want to sit here and figure it out. Come straight out and tell me." She looked at him solemnly, she wanted him more than any man she had ever known. Not only was he a great artist but he wanted her as she was. He didn't mind doing things she felt she should be doing. When she worked, he took care of the apartment and cooked. When he worked, she did. They shared everything. "Martino, with all my heart I love you, I am happy with you and feel your happiness with me. But where will we live? When will we live? Are you willing to give up all you have in the other life? Are you asking me to give up my life here and go to a world I could never understand?"

Martin had been right; she needed to know and believe he wasn't giving up anything and wasn't asking her to either. He was making a choice for a life he felt was his in a time he appreciated with a woman he adored. No sacrifice at all, it was a chance and a choice for happiness such as he had never dreamed of. He did his best to put these thoughts into words and such words that she could feel the truth in them.

When he finished he took the ring and once again bent the knee. He held the ring out to Catarina, "Catarina, when I found you, I found more than my muse I found my heart and soul. I ask you to share my life and fortune, for better or worse we can face anything so long as we have each other. I am home and while I may need to visit the other world I have lived in, my home and heart are here." During this speech Catarina had her face turned downward so he had no idea how she was taking this. Her head slowly raised as she reached out and placed the ring on her finger. Her grin illuminated her face. She leapt forward off the chair bowling Martin over and they lay on the floor kissing and holding each other.

From the doorway a shadow crossed the floor again. Pietro had returned to speak with Martin again. His voice rumbled, "You two are not normal!" Martin agreed with him and was thankful it was true.

Pietro was invited in and he and Martin discussed the future while Catarina and Marta planned the wedding. Pietro offered them a house. He was willing to purchase a home in the country even to the extent of having it built. Martin offered to pay at least half but was rebuffed. "The money for this has been saved and added to since Catarina was born. It is now time to use it." Sitting around the table everyone put in their requirements and a sketch was created.

Eventually Marta went to her apartment Pietro went to the Hospital taking Catarina with him and Martin was free to see about the next step regarding Arthur. He looked over the listing of artists Arthur had visited. He had no intention of visiting all of them. He was working it out strategically. With his Van Gogh certainly going to be called into question it would diminish his authority with some of the others. If he was found again to be in error with another key artist's work then it would make Arthur's boasts unbelievable. He would be called on to return the money from the auctions.

He ran his finger down the list. He wanted an artist that was an artist similar to himself. One who was in it for arts sake and not focused on the commercial aspects. Money was the means of allowing one to create art. He stopped when he hit on Johannes Vermeer. Here was an artist who was supposedly not appreciated in his own time. This of course was nonsense. He was well known in his time, his paintings were sold to collectors as well as patrons. Vermeer in Martins eyes was a craftsman. One who used light to bring a depth and almost photographic style to his pictures. He needed an expert to create a false painting though. His mind ran through artists who could do it then he realized he didn't want to approach someone well known but an obscure forger. He chose Han van Meegeren. For a few jewels he could get a copy accomplished well enough to fool Arthur but not so good as to fool a real expert.

Going to the present he went to a thrift store to acquire clothing he could adapt for this trip. A dark suit was found and some good black shoes fit the bill with very little need for alterations. Extensive research gave him Van Meegeren's address in the 1920's. He patched himself through and did a few quick tests. He was able to create a portal after portal leaving two open at the same time. Confident he could come and go at will he closed both portals. He checked his pockets and decided he had enough jewels for whatever Meegeren would charge.

Van Meergeren lived secluded in a large studio. When he opened the door Martin was greeted almost belligerently. "Yes?" was the perfunctory greeting. Martin explained his errand. Martin wanted an original Vermeer which he was willing to pay handsomely for. Van Meergeren ushered Martin inside and sat him down. On a large easel was a painting of the last supper. Martin was surprised that there were no sketches, pictures or models. Van Meergeren had completed it all through imagination. From a shelf he pulled down a stack of canvases which were all fake Vermeer's. He shuffled through them asking if there was one in particular Martin was seeking. "Actually I was hoping for one not currently known of. I had heard through the grapevine that you had several such items.

Van Meergeren pulled a painting similar to the woman with a pearl earing. It was a portrait of a young woman turned sideways but facing the viewer head on. Martin studied the painting carefully; it was well done and the play of light was a good approximation. Martin saw that Meergeren had used the original for the face altering it enough to make it look similar but not exact. The question was would it fool Martin. He cast his mind back to the art lessons he had taken in his youth. He had seen this portrait in the museum and as do all artists remembered it perfectly. The answer was affirmative, it would fool Arthur. Martin held out a hand with several jewels in the palm. He offered to go into town and change them or he would pass them over as they were. Bringing out a jeweler's loupe Van Meergeren examined them. Convinced of their value he took the stones and wrapping up the painting ushered Martin swiftly out the door.

Martin went down the lane to find the secluded spot he had entered in. He considered it convenient that he was using Arthurs own trips from his logs. All he had to do was change the date or time. A rumble in his stomach reminded him he was hungry. Well, a quick trip home first and then the trip to see Vermeer.

He pulled the keypad out and pushed the button for the return trip. A faint light issued from the laser but fizzled out almost immediately. He had done one test too many. As usual he had not left word where and when he was going. Nobody was at the Easel unit prepared to rescue him and he was once again up the creek without a paddle.

RESCUE ATTEMPT

"Well," He thought, "Better get to town and get some replacements." Tucking his painting under his arm he set off to town in the forlorn hope he could get a plentiful supply of AA batteries.

Back home in Italy, Catarina finished her shift and was anxious to return and see Martin. As she passed the sculpture of the nurse, she touched the forehead. She had formed a belief that this would bring her luck and it had become her habit whenever she passed it. Waving goodbye at the door she rushed out and promptly tripped over the threshold. Picking herself up she checked her surroundings and made a dash for home.

As the door flew open, she was ready to leap into Martins arms. The trouble was, Martin wasn't there. Down the stairs and across the garden she heard Marta sitting outside singing to herself. To Catarina she seemed extremely happy. The spark of jealousy never completely out, flamed and she dashed down the steps two at a time. Running up to Marta she controlled herself with difficulty. "Where is he?" She growled and the menace in her voice matched the anger in her face.

Marta automatically raised her hands defensively. "Catarina, I swear to you on the crucifix he isn't here. Suiting action to the words she repeated the pledge with her hand on the cross hanging from her neck. Catarina sat next to her. "I went home, he wasn't there. There is no letter saying where he went." Marta had heard of this happening when she had talked to Arthur after her time trip. "It is what Martino does. He goes and sometimes forgets there are others who would want to know where and when he is coming back."

Catarina admitted it wasn't the first time he had done so since meeting her but had hoped he would change. "Do you think he went home to confront Arturo?" Marta wasn't sure but if he used the easel she could find out. Opening the laptop she pulled out the list of trips. "Catarina, I don't see one for today. Wait, here's a new drop down connected to the vest. He's created a separate listing for it. It shows he's in the Netherlands." Catarina was relieved but not reassured. She went to their apartment to wait. Marta wasn't sure what she could do but followed in Catarina's wake.

After a hard day Catarina was too tired to fix herself something to eat. Marta cooked a light supper and set the table then had to prod and cajole Catarina to eat. Marta tried to figure some way to help her friend. "Look Catarina, I don't know but according to what was in the record he's actually been gone a day and a half. I think he might be having a problem, or he would have been back before you got home. I could check on him but you would have to stay at the easel and reopen the door for us." Catarina might have been sleepy but she got a sudden surge of energy. She took Marta's hand and they sped back to Marta's apartment.

Marta showed Catarina how to use the drop-down menu and to open and close the portal. Catarina did a quick test in the hope that Martin might be there waiting for them to open it. She left it open for a while in case Martin was wandering around pacing. Marta was over at the stove making a pot of coffee. Catarina came over and watched. Catarina jumped as something prodded her in the small of her back. Excited that

Martin was back she spun on her toes with arms outstretched, they wrapped around a neck and she gave the cheek a peck. When she opened her eyes. A deer was looking at her and it seemed a bit confused. Marta's eyes popped and she made a determined effort to shoo the deer back through the portal.

Being on unfamiliar territory the deer was getting more confused by the second. Marta closed the door and had Catarina herd the deer to the portal from the other side. The deer began to kick and buck knocking over chairs and tables. It leapt on the bed and broke the headboard. It jumped off the bed and did a circuit of the room knocking objects over and sending cups and plates flying. It brushed by the easel sending it teetering before taking a long leap out the portal just as the easel crashed to the floor. The portal promptly winked out.

Marta was leaning on the wall trying to catch her breath, Catarina was on the floor trying to clean up the devastation. Picking up pieces of glass and mirror her hand rested on the fallen easel. The look of terror in her eyes made Marta hurry over. They set the easel upright and accounted for what was broken. The easel itself was sturdily built and had only sustained minor cracks. Five mirrors were broken and two of the glass splitters were reduced to splinters. Catarina looked at Marta with tears in her eyes and held out her hands with the remnants. The pleading look needed no words but Marta wasn't sure what to do. She cursed herself that in the time she had been there she had never really considered studying the portal. She checked the laptop and thanked providence it was still working. Removing a mirror and a splitter from those remaining she stepped out to find replacement parts while Catarina cried herself to sleep.

Martin was also out trying to find replacement parts but not having any luck. In order to get home he needed a lead acid battery that was created in the 1920's but in this location there were none to be had. However, clay pots were in abundance. He purchased a good supply, lots of thick cork, a sharp knife, wire and copper strips. Renting a cart and he loaded it with his impromptu batteries. The hard part was finding enough vinegar to supply the electricity. As he lined up the pots. Cut cork for the tops and slid the copper through the cork he cursed he hadn't come around 1924. Dry cells would have been available and a lot less trouble than trying to do what he had to now. The vinegar was eventually supplied by a pickle plant which had a keg to spare. It had cost him the rest of his jewels and cash, but he wasn't worried about being broke. Linking his batteries, he extended two wires that he connected to his belt. He waited for the charge to build by looking around. Nearby was a deer that was sitting on its haunches with a bewildered look, as if it had had the most confusing day of its life. He grinned as he tried to figure out what could possibly have happened to it to make it so upset.

Two hours later and he was charged up enough to go home. He opened a portal setting and looked through to see an empty apartment. The deer shook its head and bolted when Martin kicked the cart with his foot sending it swiftly down the hill. Pots were hurled right and left spraying vinegar all over. The cart came to rest behind a group of bushes that effectively hid it. It wouldn't have done for Arthur to come through and find a large battery setup in the middle of nowhere. It would have given the game away. He went home and called out to Catarina.

Catarina wasn't there but from the doorway he looked over to where Marta was living and saw her returning from an outing. Stashing the painting he called out as he stepped down the stairs. Marta almost dropped the bag of mirrors and glasses. She rushed over and hugged him thankful he had found his way home. In her apartment they spoke quietly so as not to wake Catarina asleep on the bed. She showed him the damage done when the deer entered the apartment. He chuckled aloud, "So that's what he was so upset about." Together they carefully set the easel portal back to rights. After finishing off the easel Martin created a new connection on the pot battery system and hooked his vest into recharge completely. Marta took the coffee off the boil and served them both. "I'm about ready to destroy the setup in my studio. I have one more picture to deliver and then were about ready to trip up Arthur."

Marta was looking at the floor kicking some shards they had missed in the cleanup. "Martin, at the start I was all for this, now I'm not so sure." Marta looked up pleadingly, "I agree what Arthur is doing is wrong and I want to stop him, but not destroy him." Arthur lay back in his chair and sipped his coffee. "Marta, I'm not as hard hearted as you seem to think I am. All I plan on doing is making his reputation questionable. The first Van Gogh is a fraud, most of the rest can be authentic, we have one more that is going to be a fraud as well. This means that his reputation will suffer, and he'll have to return some of the money. Marta, I want to talk with you about the future. Yours's and the galleries." Marta pricked up her ears then let out a screech as she was showered in coffee. Catarina had woken at the sound of Martin's voice and flung herself at him, his cup went flying with the aforementioned result.

Grabbing a rag Marta cleaned herself up and asked Martin to continue once Catarina finished welcoming him home. Martin recommenced with Catarina on his lap, her arms around his neck and head on his shoulder. "Once Arthurs reputation tumbles the gallery is going to take a serious hit. I think you might be a better lead for the place. Once the value goes down would you be willing to buy it?" Marta gave it careful consideration. "I might, I make plenty and have invested most of it. That's why I was in such a panic about the tablet. I could probably afford it if I take out all my holdings. It's a shame you won't be around to place your work into it." She smiled warmly. Martin had an ace up his sleeve. "Marta, how much did they value the statue of the nurse for. I mean for the insurance." Marta went through the information on her tablet. "Seven Million, That's actually rather low. For a work like that but I guess since the artist was "unknown" he wouldn't have been able to insure it for more."

She paused and thought about possibilities. "Martin, I think I understand what you're driving at. You provide statues that are classical from this time, we "locate them" and then sell them. It isn't going to be that easy. Italy especially is getting uptight about items from here being sold overseas. They're losing their heritage and are starting to keep a tight hold on them." Martin did some considerations of his own. What if I seeded a monastery in say Illinois. We find one that has been abandoned then seed the basement with statues. You send a team to explore it and get clearance to keep anything you find." Marta sat upright, "I know Arthur did that a couple of times when he was trying to mingle your sculptures with older ones to raise their value."

She perked up considerably, "I think that could work. When I go back I can do a look through his files and redo the paperwork. How soon could you have enough to sell in bulk, say eight to start with." Martin asked for a few years to ensure he produced his best works." Marta was beginning to get excited. "I can keep the Gallery going for a while the same way we have been. Under new management we should be able to bring some artists back." Marta and Martin clasped hands and Catarina, not wishing to be left out, placed hers on top.

Martin grabbed his vest and ambled back to his and Catarina's apartment. There he changed and left to place the painting with Vermeer in preparation for Arthur's arrival. He returned disgruntled; Vermeer was not willing to put a false painting amongst his works. Martin was sitting at the table strumming his fingers when another thought crossed his mind. He called down to Marta to come up and bring Catarina with her. They came running. "Vermeer wasn't keen on testing Arthur, so I want to try and accomplish it another way. Marta, look up the Gallery and keep an eye out for this picture." He placed the picture on a chair so she could take a picture then grabbing a few jewels, slipped on his vest and left. Within moments he returned sans picture and in very good humor. Marta was still searching and saw that the painting he had just released was sold by Arthur for one point five million." Martin looked almost dejected at what he considered a low price. Marta pulled up a small painting by Vermeer that had sold recently for ten dollars. "O.k. were set then. Time to go pull the plug on Arthur."

PLANS AND PROMISES

Back in Marta's apartment they opened the easel, locked the door, shuttered the windows, and programed the portal onto the studio. Martin had set the date to right before he had lost control of the primary portal. In the studio he handed out cotton gloves and shoe protectors. Leaving the portal open they took everything from the studio. Martin realized quickly there was no way to store it all at his new home. He used the vest and purchased a house in Wisconsin. It was out and away from everything and had been for sale for a long time, he was able to get it cheap. One thing about having a time machine at your disposal is that you can take care of everything that would take months in a matter of minutes. Everyone came through for an inspection and agreed it would do as a safe place. Martin felt it would make also make a good studio if he ever wanted to come back sometime. Opening a new portal, they transferred the entire studio to the house. The tricky part was transporting the original portal through. Catarina was called away from the door where she had been keeping watch to help lift. Once through she rushed back to the door to continue the lookout.

Everything gone, Catarina insisted they sweep the floor and dust the shelves. She stood with hands on hips and a firm look in her eyes. She just couldn't allow them to leave it in this state. Marta and Martin shrugged and did it. Once at the house in Wisconsin they setup the portal to appear just outside the studio. Martin went outside and brought in three fair-sized stones. Handing one each to Marta and Catarina they all threw them through the large plate glass window. An alarm sounded as they closed the portal.

Sitting at the table with a glass of wine, they used laptop and tablet to keep abreast of the results of their adventure. Not much in the news about the break in at the studio. Martin had filed an insurance claim for fifteen million for stolen sculptures. According to him the studio was full of precious works of art and had been used for storage for months. Marta was disgusted but Martin thought it was hilarious. He went back in time to the day before and renewed his studios insurance providing a picture time and date stamped for the evening right before the robbery. This was sent to the insurance company. Arthur was not given the fifteen million. Arthur was brought in for questioning regarding the claim.

He was released but word got around quickly about the false claim. Martin sent an anonymous letter to the person who had purchased the Van Gogh suggesting that it be authenticated again. Inspected at Sotheby's again and also by several independent experts, it was discovered to be a fake. The documents were again examined and considered unreliable. Suddenly all the works Arthur had put up for sale were being called into question. Local artworks were considered sound. It was only the ones that he claimed as newly found works that seemed to be a problem. When the Vermeer was examined, it was found to be a forgery and they were even able to discover the forger due to certain characteristics, especially the eyes. Arthur closed the gallery and set about trying to locate the thieves who had stolen the portal. He placed adds in everything from Craigslist to small town papers locally. He even offered large sums for its return with no questions asked. No one ever answered his ads.

Arthur was growing desperate. He purchased a worktable, computer and all the accoutrements he could remember to try and reconstruct it. When he tried to purchase the laser, he found his account had been frozen. Marta was becoming uneasy. "Martin, you've had your revenge, if it was revenge you wanted. Let's not drive him to suicide." Martin nodded agreement. He was beginning to become worried they had pushed things too far already. The problem was what to do now. Martin homed in on Arthur working frantically on the portal. Without Martin he was having a hard time understanding the means to create a hologram which was the basis for the portal. He was breaking mirrors and glass as frustration mounted. His phone rang and was hurled at the wall. With cut hands wrapped in cloth, his hair in disarray and his eyes red from lack of sleep, Martin felt it was time to intervene.

Stepping through the portal into Arthur's apartment he was almost overwhelmed by the stench. Arthur hadn't bathed in a week, and it appeared he hadn't changed his clothes either. Martin came up behind Arthur and placed a hand gently on his shoulder. Arthur swung on his heel and knocked Martin out with a single shot to the jaw. Martin came to hearing Arthur's pleas for him to come round. He felt tears on his cheeks falling from Arthurs eyes. Martin pushed himself up to a sitting position and leant against the wall. Holding his jaw, he blurted out, "Nice to see you too!"

Arthur sat on the floor leaning his back against the wall as well. He was weak from exertion and worry. He looked over at Martin not sure if he should be relieved or concerned or downright scared. "Pal, you wouldn't believe the things that are happening to me." Martin leaned forward and looked across at Arthur. His brows closed together and his voice lowered. "The hell I wouldn't." The tone in Martins voice made Arthur sit up and the look on his face was one he'd never seen before. Martin hitched a thumb over his shoulder towards the bathroom. Get cleaned up and then we'll go home and talk.

Arthur scurried to do as he was told. Soaped and under hot water he considered the change in Martin. Arthur had always been the one in charge, but it seemed the tide had turned. And how the hell did he have a portal. He had said his was destroyed! Clean and in fresh clothes he saw an open portal and was pushed through. In Marta's apartment in Italy Arthur saw a trio of very upset faces sitting in judgement. He sat down and for the moment was not very anxious to meet whatever they had in store.

Martin folded his hands on the table. The earnestness in his voice held Arthur's attention more than ranting and raving could have. "Arthur, you asked me if I know what has been happening to you, I know very well. I'm responsible for most of it." Arthur leapt to his feet knocking over the table. "You! Do you realize how much trouble you've gotten me into. I've always been your friend, I sold your pieces even when I knew I wasn't going to get anything out of them. You owe me, do you hear me? You owe me." He gasped for breath, "What kind of sick joke are you pulling, you used me. Do you have any idea of how that feels?"

A smile played on Martins face. They were already at the point he wanted, and it hadn't taken long. He looked up at

Arthur who was breathing fire. He got up and pushed Arthur back into his chair. Now he was up and looking down at Arthur. "You're DAMN right I do. You've been using me since we started. How much from the sales of my works have you been keeping. Over half on most and still had the gall to charge commission on the little you gave me. I'd sure as hell say that's being used." His face registered the anger he felt inside and it was frightening.

"Then you took my machine and used it to make yourself rich by getting the early works of some of the greatest artists for nothing. You created false paperwork to try and legitimize your sales, but you didn't know enough about the classics to recognize fake work when you saw it did you." He pounded his fist on the table, "How many other artists have you cheated. How many other people have you used." He sat down, his voice was becoming hoarse. Martin still had enough fire in him to be ironical, "Alright Edmond, what do you plan on doing with me."

Martin understood the reference to Edmond Dantès and his revenge mission. Marta felt it time to intercede, "Arthur, you must admit Edmond, I mean, Martin is right. You got so bad you even took shots at us. What happens next depends a lot on what you do now." She looked at Martin who had calmed down but was still visibly seething inside. Getting up she paced around the room eventually sitting next to the easel. With a crafty smile she entered in new coordinates. Setting the open, close, open timer, she quietly passed through and reemerged within a short time. In her hand was a small envelope and a stack of bills. She sat on the bed listening. She realized things were progressing as she thought it would. It was going to take a hell of a shock to get Arthur in line. She looked at Martin's red face and realized it was time.

She loaded the portal into a steamship first class cabin. Walking around the table she whispered in Martins ear. She approached Arthur and stuck the cash and envelope in his pocket. "It's time we put you out of the way for a bit." Arthur was in shock as Martin kicked him through the portal chair and all. The portal closed as he went through.

Arthur slammed into the bed and leapt up. Looking around at the comfortable surroundings he considered himself fortunate that even with the attitude he had shown they still couldn't do him any real harm. "They just want me out of the way while they fix things up so I can go home." He pulled a cigar from a box on the dresser and rolled it as he toasted the end. Sitting in an overstuffed leather chair he leafed through the bills. Enough there for a good while. From above the bed a portal opened and a tuxedo dropped down with cufflinks and polished shoes. Dressing fastidiously, he brushed his hair with a silver handled brush amongst the elegant toilet fixtures. Looking into the mirror he smoothed his mustache and gave a twirl to his forelock. Elegantly attired and carefully shaved he felt he had never cut so dashing a figure.

He strolled into the Dining Room and found his place at a large table with eight other passengers. The lady on his right was Mrs. Margaret Brown from New York. She was pleasant, well-spoken and had a wonderful sense of humor. On his left was a Mr. William Carter who spoke of nothing except polo and bored Arthur to tears. Dinner was a sumptuous affair of oysters, roast duck, applesauce, roast squab, and Waldorf pudding for dessert. Full and in an excellent humor he wandered around the ship taking in the luxury he had always wanted to be surrounded by. The sea air filled his lungs. He had a short interlude in the smoking room where he enjoyed several high quality cigars and talked about art with the other smokers. As the evening wore on, he began to get chilly and then sleepy. He hadn't had a good night's sleep in what seemed like years.

He stripped off and lay on his bed admiring the deep rich paneling and polished brass fittings. When he had been kicked so abruptly through the portal, he hadn't expected anything so posh. He laughed to think they considered they were punishing him. What fools! He edged down deeper under the blanket and covers. The pillow beneath his head cradled him comfortably. He turned down the light as the gentle rocking of the ship lulled him to sleep.

The sound of someone hammering on his door woke him. Irritated, he donned his trousers and looking at the clock saw it was only 0200! He opened the door to see people running to the deck. He quickly finished dressing and strode wrathfully onto the deck. Someone would pay if they decided to do a drill this early in the morning. The cold air shocked him to full wakefulness. He saw people lined up to enter lifeboats as the crew tried to keep order. Looking down the deck towards the bow he saw the tip of an iceberg in the ships lights.

He had never paid any attention to what ship he was on. With the realization he was on the Titanic he became weak and pale. He was going to push through the line but was grabbed by a crewman and practically thrown back into the line. "Women and children first sir, you might just as well hang back." Sweating profusely despite the cold he ran around the deck hoping to find a better chance of rescue somewhere else.

Dashing back and forth became hazardous as the ship slowly tilted. He grabbed onto a railing seeking higher ground. Now at a forty-five degrees angle, he could barely stand, his shoes were slippery. He was holding onto the railing so tight it was cutting into his hands. His arms ached and his fingers were losing sensation. Cold and the splash of water were freezing him. Panicking as he felt the last grip of his fingers loosen, he went sliding down the deck hurtling towards the cold dark water below. He held his breath and waited for the icy plunge.

+

RESOLUTION

Just at the point of entering the water a portal burst open in front of him and quickly closed. He flopped onto the apartment floor and bounced. The look of stark terror was still frozen on his face. It took more than one bracing shot of brandy for him to return to his senses. His eyes were wild and his face still pale. He shivered but it wasn't only from the cold chill of the night he had left. He tried to speak but all he could do was stammer. Never in his life had he experienced anything as terrifying. He looked with wide eyes at the faces surrounding him. He hadn't expected them to do anything so extreme. His mind couldn't comprehend how much he had hurt them to cause them to do something like that. A thought that made him shudder suddenly crossed his mind. They could do that to him at anytime from anywhere. He was at their mercy and if he didn't toe the line, they could bring him to somewhere or to somewhen even worse. His head dropped and he acknowledged defeat. Martin brought out a sheaf of papers. The last was a note making Marta his partner.

Martin looked at Arthur with probably more sympathy than was his due. It really wasn't in his nature to be mean or vengeful even though he had a terrible temper when concentrating on his works. "Arthur we've arranged things so you can go back. With Marta as the senior partner the Gallery will have a new but familiar face. It will give you time to rebuild your reputation *and perspective.*" Arthur looked up a beaten man. He signed the paper giving Marta an equal share but fifty one percent control. He hadn't lost much really when he thought about it. His reputation could be carefully crafted better than before. He could work out a deal with Marta and take on the newer, modern artists while Marta took control of the classics. It might work out as the best of both worlds. Catarina was in tears at the thought of Marta leaving but Marta reminded her that they could always come up or bring her down. It had been an experience seeing great works of art being created and one she would never forget.

Marta took Catarina outside into the garden. It was a cool day, and the sun was hidden behind a bank of clouds. Flowers that all had a place in a hospital pharmacopeia bloomed around them. "Catarina, I've begun to think of you as a sister and I would miss you if we didn't see each other often. Martins got a nice place in the future and being secluded it might be interesting for you to visit once in a while. I might be able to talk to Martin into making me a vest so I can come back whenever I'm free." Catarina cheered up and decided to try and see if Martin could make the vest immediately. She even considered having him make one for herself. She thought it odd that the idea of going to the future or past had come to her so naturally. Time was just another place that was different. Really no better or worse than now when you compared them.

Martin came out and offered to help Marta pack but was sternly informed that she and Catarina would be able to do it. For a while the sounds from her apartment were of singing and laughter as Marta got packed and ready to go home. Martin and Arthur were called in when everything had to be moved. The fact that Marta had left some things here pleased both Martin and Catarina. It meant she would be coming back.

Arthur was taken home to his apartment. Martin came through to help him straighten it up and get him back on his feet. On the dining table were forms and restitution owed to the people that had purchased the false paintings. Arthur tackled the pile of forms and wrote checks with a growing disquiet. He had a great deal of money going out and almost none coming in from the Gallery. He hoped the announcement of it being under new management would bring business back. He was amazed at how quickly his fortunes had fallen, then when he remembered he had an acquaintance with a time machine it all made sense.

When all was completed, he handed Martin a glass of whiskey, "I hope someday you will be able to consider me a friend again." They drank and Martin looked at Arthur long and hard. What Arthur had done to him hurt. There was no getting over that but what he had done to him hurt too. He felt it would be a long time before either one would be in a position to trust the other. He patted Arthur's shoulder and pulling the keypad from his pocket went home.

Catarina had his trunk of electrical equipment open at the table. A leather vest was laid out and the two pieces of Kevlar were above it. She was sitting at the table expectantly. She tapped the vest, "You need to make one for Marta." Martin agreed but wanted something to eat first. She offered to get him food but only if he started right away. Laying out the Kevlar and covering it with metal he started the process of building another vest portal. Catarina returned with a basket of food and prepared him dinner. Ducking into the closet she came out changed for work. "Gotta go, I'll be back in the morning." She kissed him quickly, got to the door and returned for a proper kiss. Martin continued to work on the vest but with his mind elsewhere.

The next morning Marta was in possession of her own portal vest. Martin handed it over with an admonition that she not let Arthur know of it. From then on Marta traveled back and forth effortlessly, becoming at home in both worlds. Together they worked out a series of sculptures which would be "seeded" in the basement of the monastery. Martin began to work on those as well as the sculptures he was commissioned for. The first sculpture completed for the Sistine Chapel was so admired that commissions were coming thick and fast. He had to move out of Michelangelo's studio and take on one of his own. By the end of the year he was beginning to question his determination to be a classical artist exclusively.

He began to miss the challenge of art that was a combination of classical art mixed with electronics. He began to work in the present also, he wanted a piece to be placed at the Gallery. It had been a while since he had placed anything and requests for a new piece were being asked for. Using the head and plastic shadow piece as inspiration he worked on a large sculpture that was going to be his masterpiece. Standing at 8'x4'x6" it was simply a white board. What didn't show were thousands of plastic sheets on runners that could be inserted, retracted, moved and inserted again. The frame held the lights set on a series of switches. From the center and extended out was a small projector. He worked on an automated patch board to control everything.

The first test was completed within a month. A picture of a Chicago street scene was projected. Thin slivers of plastic were extended and lights would turn on in succession. It made the image come to life. Shadows extended making movement in a static picture. He worked picture after picture. Waterfalls went from a picture into flowing motion. Pastoral fields came to life with grass waving in the breeze as clouds floated past. He tried to have at least a 10 picture series.

The final was a complete shadow story against a blank background. Once programed he sat Catarina down to view it. It was the story of Romeo and Juliet done complete as shadows. It took Catarina a while to understand how to read a shadow story but once she understood the moving shadows had her enthralled. Martin stained the frame and sprayed the glass to reduce reflection. Transportation was becoming a logistical nightmare until he remembered he could pass it through using the portal. Laying it on its side on carpet rollers, he projected the portal for night when the Gallery was closed. Rolling it in he placed it into the holding area on the first floor and had one spotlight left on it.

Marta arrived at the Gallery early as was her custom. Sitting at the large desk she went over the floor and picture changes as well as the items that were being returned to the artists and the artists who were requesting inclusion to the gallery. It had been a while since they had one of Martins unique pieces and she wished she had one to kick things off again. His pieces brought in crowds. Walking downstairs she saw a light on in the holding room. Cursing the wasteful person who left the large light burning she saw in the light Martins present. The cord was plugged in. She searched for the switch to turn it on finally finding it in a recess of the frame. Pulling a chair in front she sat down comfortably waiting anxiously to see what Martin had created.

A shadow was created in the top right corner. It formed into a bird that flew down landing at the base before fading away. The pictures were shown first as flat projections then brought to life, in each somewhere was the bird sometimes sleeping on a limb, other times fluttering around the picture. It became a game to find it. Finally came the pièce de résistance. She watched in awe as the story of Romeo and Juliet played out silently before her. So enraptured was she that she never saw the other employees who were gathered behind her watching just as captivated. When it was over the applause startled her, nearly giving her a heart attack. Several people had tears in their eyes. She watched as space was swiftly cleared on the main floor to make room for the latest Martin piece. Lights in the gallery were dimmed and the pictures were given spotlights only.

The piece Martin had created was a huge success. For months the Gallery was swamped with viewers. Newspapers and television shows were arriving daily. Martin was often requested to speak about his current and past works. The Gallery was becoming lucrative again as unique artists wanted to place their work in the company of an artist with such a unique vision. It was becoming difficult for Martin to keep his dual life separate. He requested Marta and Arthur to sell it promising several shadow sculptures of a much smaller size each projecting a different Shakespeare play. The day of the sale was arriving. It was becoming obvious from the requests for tickets the gallery was too small to accommodate the sale. It was held in a nearby park.

Martin and Catarina arrived and were received on the podium to thunderous applause. For the benefit of all who were there, the picture was placed under the shade of a canopy and turned on. On two side screens the view was enlarged. Finished, the crowd once again erupted in approbation. Catarina, watching the crowds' emotions change and flow with the shadow play, saw firsthand how Martin's works of art moved people. He was more than a classist but a brilliant engineer who could create something wonderful using something so elusive as shadows. She sat there filled with pride and admiration, plus a tinge of jealousy. She was determined that someday, somehow, she would be the one to receive the accolades. Somehow, she would find her niche and make her mark.

Martin stood and gave his speech about the picture, thanked everyone for coming and introduced Catarina as his muse. She blushed a fiery red and discreetly kicked him for embarrassing her, but the applause she received she adored. Something like this would never happen in her own time. "Perhaps there's a place for me in this time?" She wondered. Martin wondered how the auctioneer could make any sense of the bidding. Never had he seen it so swift. Cards rose and fell in a flurry of motion and the auctioneer's words were so quick he couldn't follow them, the bidding slowed at seven million and stopped at seven million four hundred thousand. After commission to the gallery the remainder that he received floored him. He could change the money to jewels and go back and purchase a larger home for Catarina after the wedding. He turned her to discuss the possibility when, to his dismay, she wasn't there. The crowd was streaming out of the park and Martin was afraid she had gotten lost in the shuffle. He asked security to see if they could find her while he raced around the park.

PROSPECTS

After several circuits of the park, he found a section he had missed. A small children's park was partially hidden from his view by some bushes. Winded and leaning against a tree to catch his breath he saw a familiar figure sitting in a sandbox. Relief flowed through him as he walked quietly up to her. She was seated in the moist sand and was modeling a head of himself. Hearing him despite his attempt at stealth she half turned and showed for his critique the sand sculpture she had been molding, a bust of himself.

"I love it, it's a shame we can't take it with us. When we get home were going to have to set up space in the new house for your studio." Her ears perked up at the sound of a studio for herself, but she suddenly looked dejected at the thought of moving houses. "I love our apartment; do you need a larger place?" Martin shrugged. The apartment was just fine with him, but a little more space wouldn't come amiss. Catarina leapt to her feet, her foot ruining her sculpture, "Just buy the whole building and we can make our room as big as we want!" Kissing her, he agreed and would change money into gold or jewels and see about purchasing the apartment building as soon as possible. He marveled at what she considered a simple compromise. Returning to the platform Martin wondered about the possibility of finding a taxi.

Marta had waited. They returned to the gallery in high spirits. Inside Marta had a small party going. Champagne was flowing and people were singing and dancing, Catarina was trying to do some of the dances but couldn't understand what people were doing. Eventually she wandered back and laid down. When Martin found her, she was sound asleep in a couple of chairs. He said goodbye and found a secluded spot to open the portal in.

It took Martin a year to convert all his money into exchangeable jewels. The year had been an exhausting one. He and Marta opted for a small wedding then worked with Pietro on small place in the country as a home and studio. He purchased the Apartment building as promised and offered to move a couple of tenants to new accommodations with a refund and bonus as incentive.

Catarina was happy to be able to spread the rooms out a little. Marta had her apartment ready at all times and the easel portal was moved back upstairs into Martin and Caterina's quarters. One room had been set aside to house the portal and was where Martin painted. Catarina had most of the rest of the room for experimenting on different modes of art.

Marta visited often, usually bringing ideas for Martin's sculptures or paintings. He had begun a large selection of religious sculptures. Working on his latest piece he was interrupted. A monk had opened the door and was hesitant about interrupting the artist at work. He approached Martin respectfully. Martin liked the look of the monk. Though obviously well on in years he carried himself upright and had an aura of authority. Martin assumed he was the head of some order.

The monk excused himself and looked over the selection Martin had been working on. These were to be salted in the United States at the site of missions that had long been abandoned. There was a dozen created already and he had decided on doing a few more. The monk looked in wonder at the impassioned look in the faces. The smooth suppleness of the muscles, there was a feeling to them that he hadn't seen in the other artists he had visited.

"Maestro, I have seen your sculpture while visiting the Sistine Chapel. We are opening many missions throughout the new world. Would you be willing to sell these to grace our missions?" The monk spoke with a heavy Spanish accent. The Spanish were the first to create missions in the United States. Martin looked on this as an opportunity of a lifetime. The work of salting would be done for him only he needed to know where his pieces would be located.

"Padre, It would be an honor for my works to grace your missions. For this reason, I am willing to give them to you at no cost. This is provided that you send word to me of where my statues will be. I have a desire to travel to the new world some day and seeing my works already in place would give me great joy." The monk excused himself and returned with a map that showed the locations for the new missions. Martin made a copy of the map and returned the original. The monk left to make arrangements for the sculptures to be transported and shipped.

In the time between sale and pickup, he crated and protected his works with plenty of straw and blankets. He was ecstatic once they were all headed out. His next mission was to send the map to Marta and Arthur so the work of discovery could begin. The thought that this was being done without deception was a relief. He opened a portal and placed the map ready for Marta and Arthur when they arrived.

Marta arrived first as she always had. Old habits die hard and she had most of the work done by the time the morning shift arrived. Arriving at the desk Arthur had originally used she went over the paperwork for the day. Some she passed over to Arthur's desk for when he arrived. Last of the papers was a map of missions. Martins unsteady scrawl was added on a post it note. "My works are in all of these. Some may be found if searched for. I did some preliminary research, most are in ruins and will need to be dug up. From what I can tell it's a better way then seeding a single place." Marta considered the time and expense and decided to pass this off onto Arthur. It would be added into his "research" of the artist known simply as Martino. A student of Michelangelo's who branched out on his own. This would rebuild Arthur's reputation.

Arthur took the list and called into a group of archaeologists at Berkeley California. Using students meant the work was cheaper and they got credit for any finds. He triangulated the meeting point and called them into action to begin the dig. He booked a flight out and grabbed his traveling bag from the closet. He was eager to rebuild his reputation and get back on the right side in the art world again. His work on Martino would repair a lot of damage. He hoped so anyway. Waving farewell to Marta he headed to O'Hare Airport and was soon whisked off on his adventure.

Over the weeks of digging the mission gradually became visible. This mission had apparently been burnt down after the missionaries were run out by the local community, a number of religious artifacts were contained in the cellar where they had been stored in the hopes of protecting them. Careful digging produced a sculpture that was laying down next to a large cross. This was what he had come for and the small bird carved into the base confirmed that this was a Martino. At a wooden folding desk, he wrote out a report to be used by the school on this particular find. The sculpture was photographed and sent to the gallery along with a few paintings. The rest of the finds would go to Berkley. Seated at the desk he talked to the professor who had accompanied the students. She was looking over the students as they scraped at the finds carefully photographing them as they were slowly uncovered. "I don't know how you found out about this but if you hear about more, I'd appreciate you letting us in on them." Arthur pulled the photocopy from his satchel and laid it out for her to see. "We believe this was created by the head of the missions sent out here. This was the first dig and we'll be using satnav and geos to check on the rest. Once we determine the state and definitive locations we'll better understand the accuracy of this map." He looked up and saw such enthusiasm that he was catching some of it himself. "Tell you what, There's a decent restaurant about ten miles away that might make a change from the field rations. What say we take everyone out and dinners on me."

At the Bohemian Gardens restaurant, they packed the place and Arthur told everyone that they could order whatever they wanted, Professor Cynthia Grunther amended that with the stipulation nothing over twenty dollars. She thanked Arthur for inviting them all for dinner. "We'll I wasn't sure you'd accept an invitation with myself alone so I figured fifteen chaperones would make you feel safer." She laughed softly and sipped her wine. "You know, I'm glad we finally have gotten to meet. Your works previous to your recent trouble were wonderful, I know the Art department used many of your writeups in the class. Would it offend you if I asked, why?"

Arthur momentarily bristled but was immediately glad to have a moment to talk to her about it. Not to justify himself but to explain his actions. "I was a fool, an ambitious fool. I found one piece that I truly believed was authentic. I saw discrepancies but was so thrilled at the possibility of finding a new work that I brushed them off. The problem was that there was no line of ownership. I was a fool and created one. Then others came my way, these were genuine and there were no discrepancies to shake my faith. After a while I got cocky and didn't research enough. I got sloppy, then I got caught in my errors. I lost everything." He hung his head in humiliation. She reached over and patted his hand.

"It's happened to some of the best in all fields. Arthur, there is no such thing as too big to fail. It happed to myself early in my career. Now I'm cautious and do my own research. I've worked hard to rebuild my reputation and so will you." Arthur looked up into sympathetic eyes. His fingers intwined with hers and they reached a mutual silent understanding. How long they were lost in each other's eyes can best be explained by the rest of the group finishing eating and congregating by the exit. With one voice they called out, "We'd like to leave please." To the amusement of staff and customers alike. Red faced, Cynthia and Arthur rose. Arthur paid the bill as Cynthia brought her students onto the van. The ribbing continued on the bus as Arthur and Cynthia were serenaded with "Arthur and Cynthia sitting in a tree K. I. S. S. I. N. G. etc.

Back at the site everyone secured their section and hopped into the tents. A head popped out as the last one went to bed, "Don't stay up late canoodling you two!" Cynthia put her head in her hands, "I'm never going to live this down am I" Arthur put his arm around her and she scootched closer. Looking up she talked about the constellations visible and their history. Suddenly she stopped talking and held his hand and simply looked. By morning they were still seated side by side at the picnic table. Students came out and lit a fire for coffee and washups. Arthur roused himself and assisted in the morning preparations. The statue and paintings were due to be picked up by 1300 and he was going to leave for the airport by four. After the pickup was made and the statue was on its way, he escorted Cynthia out of sight and earshot.

"Cynthia, I'm glad I had a chance to see you and talk to you in person. Please believe I have been totally honest with you about my," He paused, he tried to find a way to say something about his behavior that didn't sound as bad as it was. "I can't find a way to soften what I did so we'll let it pass and move on. I've been fond of you since our first communications. Since meeting you I understand why I was attracted to you from the start. I hope my honesty and diligence in rectifying things will make you think less badly of me."

She blushed as she took him in her arms and kissed him with as much warmth as she could. More was said and an understanding deep and confidential arose between them. As they walked to the waiting taxi she reminded him of their pledge. "If you ever feel your train is going off the track call me and I'll be there to get you back on the right one." He got in and rolled down the window. She leaned in and kissed him then waved as he was driven off site to applause from the students. He smiled as he sunk into the back seat. It might just be a good year after all.

FINALE'

Martin worked diligently on the pieces that he had promised the gallery. Each one conveyed a different scene from a Shakespeare play. He had his own corner of the gallery where his new pieces received constant attention. He settled for creating a new extravagant piece every six months. This gave him a break from his classical pieces, and all were done at his studio in Wisconsin. They began to become used to the double life he and Christina led. Somedays in Italy of the past sometimes in the present in Wisconsin. He took Christina to Art Museums all over. She soaked up culture like a sponge and used it in creating her attempts at art. She was learning the art of sculpting and her creations were improving. She was using Martin as her muse and sometimes her father. Her latest sculpture was of her father bent over a patient. Martin was impressed and promised to cast it for her when it was completed. He was tempted to see if it was still around in the future. Of course, if not, he could always see that it was.

Arthur was sitting in the Gallery office doing a writeup on the newest Martino find. His findings now had corroboration through Berkley which worked with the gallery on excavating monasteries in search of artifacts. Martin assisted by laying a paper trail where he left definitive proof of his existence. Letters of ownership on the studio, correspondences with patrons, and of course his sculptures which were spoken of almost as much as Michelangelo's. Arthur found an interesting story in a book on Leonardo Da Vinci. It appeared that Michelangelo and Martino had created a robot after hearing about one Leonardo created. Everything was operated off of gears and levers and weighted ropes. Martin and Michelangelo decided to one up Leonardo and created a clockwork spring to move theirs more smoothly.

From an excerpt in Lost Legends of Leonardo by Ponce D. Leon *"It was reported that On June 14th, 1657, The team of Martino and Michelangelo challenged Leonardo Da Vinci to a robot duel. The rules were that the machines were to be programed in advance and then allowed to continue until they ran out. Leonardo had upgraded his machine for the event and brought it to the square." Martin and Michelangelo were already there, their creation gleamed in the morning sun. Leonardo and his team uncrated his and the two machines were spaced apart by three feet. The two combatants faced off, Leonardo and Martino wound up their units.*

A member of the crowd was brought in to act as referee. "At the word of command both men will engage their machines." He cried to be heard over the crowd. Both men stood at the ready. The referee gave the command and both machines were set in motion.

Both knights were programed for thrust and parry and would often make contact with each other in loud clanging bangs. It seemed as though both were evenly programed; it was going to be simply a matter of which ran down first. Martino saw Leonardo push another button behind his unit and it started walking forward. Michelangelo was shouting "Il Fallo, Il Fallo!" The referee seemed to think everything was going smoothly and no yellow card was shown. The program on Martino's knight had just committed five parries in a row and was now committed to thrusts.

As Michelangelo's knight came in range Martino's performed a thrust which sent Leonardo's spinning. It fell down leaving Martino and Michelangelo as winners. A roar went up from the crowd and Michelangelo and Martino were carried on shoulders back to Martino's studio. Martino checked behind to see their robot also held aloft and coming along too. In the distance they could see Leonardo Da Vinci kicking pieces of his robot all over the square.

In his studio he and Michelangelo toasted to the success of their challenge. Michelangelo encouraged Martin to continue experimenting with robotics. It would make a change he said and keep him fresh. When Michelangelo left Martin worked on a painting he wanted to give to Catarina for a present. It was approaching their anniversary and he wanted a surprise for her.

In her half of the studio she was working on her present for Martin. She planned on finishing it tonight and giving it to him in the morning. It was a small sculpture but as detailed as she could make it. She made a plaster cast and then filled the mold. When completed she painted it as realistically as she could.

In the present Martino's statue arrived in great state and was cleaned carefully then installed in the section reserved for Martino's works. Arthur was taking pictures and doing writeups on this hitherto unappreciated artist. As details became corroborated his reputation slowly recovered. He was becoming an asset again and he and Marta were slowly becoming reconciled. He kept in touch with Cynthia and flew out periodically to be with her. He planned on getting engaged hopefully before the year was out.

Marta was excited about Martins latest masterpiece. Continuing with the theme of shadow art he had created his most unusual piece. It was eight feet long and two feet high. When turned on, it was a shadow train trip from California to Chicago. The train started out as a steam train and gradually transitioned during the trip to the most modern train in existence. The moment the first writeups went out the Gallery was again crowded with viewers who stayed for hours. It was decided to move Martins' work to one of the side buildings to free up space for buyers. Offers were coming in all the time as people tried to inveigle them to sell it before the auction.

Martin and Catarina were seated having their usual light breakfast and exchanging gifts when Marta arrived. Catarina was enthusiastic at having her friend there to celebrate with them. Martins painting was of Catarina of course, but with her exactly as she was. It was almost photographic in its details and Catarina was in awe of it. His symbol of a bird was seen as a pin on her blouse. Out of curiosity Marta brought out her tablet and did a google search. It was in the Louvre Museum not far from the Mona Lisa.

Catarina went to a cupboard and brought out her gift. It was small and wrapped in linen. She laid it carefully in front of Martin and sat in eager expectation of his response. Carefully unwrapping the bundle he unveiled a small figure of a baby. In detail it might have been alive and it looked very much like a small version of himself. He turned pale as he looked from the sculpture to Catarina. His questioning look was eloquent. She nodded in agreement with what she felt were his thoughts. She was indeed turning into a great artist, she was also pregnant with their greatest masterpiece.